DEATH AND EGGNOG

SUGAR CREEK

BOOK FIVE

NOVA WALSH

TWO WORLDS PRESS

CHAPTER ONE

Christmas Eve fell as balmy as April.

My fellow Texan, O. Henry, was no stranger to the plight of us Sugar Creek residents during the holidays. The weather never wants to match our festive moods, no matter how many Christmas ornaments, twinkling lights, or sparkly tinsel we hang. More often than not we show up to Christmas dinner in shorts and flip-flops.

But despite the current uncooperative sunny weather, Primrose House was abuzz with holiday activity. My Aunt Meg, who owned the B&B, and her faithful helper Maria, were busy hanging holly and garland around the front room that doubled as a lobby and check-in area and I was stringing lights around the big Christmas tree that took up one corner near the unused fireplace as we prepared for guests to arrive. Bing Crosby serenaded us in the background, making me nostalgic as I went about my tasks.

After I finished with the string of lights, I stepped back to admire my handiwork and then checked my watch. I had plenty of work to do in the kitchen still, but I knew Aunt Meg was pressed for time too, and I wanted to help out as much as I could.

Mondays are usually quiet around Primrose House. Most of

the guests leave on Sunday and it's a time when Aunt Meg and Maria like to put things back to rights in a slower fashion. But this Monday, the B&B was a flurry of activity because we were expecting bona fide celebrities to arrive later in the day.

"Are you all ready for the big arrival?" I asked her as I looked around the room. There were ornaments and holly and strings of light everywhere, but it was an organized chaos. "Or is there anything else I can help you with before I get back to the kitchen?"

"No, honey. We're good," Aunt Meg replied. Her face was a mixture of excitement and jitters. Katherine Kirby, a local girl turned broadway star, would be gracing the Sugar Creek theater with her performing prowess for the town's annual Christmas play and pageant. I didn't know how they'd coerced her into agreeing to participate, but no doubt someone had called in a serious favor—or blackmailed with old secrets—to get the star to come back to Sugar Creek for the performance.

We'd never had anyone even close to as famous as Katherine Kirby stay at Primrose House, and I knew it would be a big step up in her business.

"Maria and I have got it from here if you need to get back to the kitchen."

I nodded and picked up a few stray scraps of tinsel that littered the old wood floor as I started back toward the kitchen. But before I made it out of the room, I spied a long black car pull into the parking lot of Primrose House and my eyes grew wide.

"Looks like your big star is here!" I said as my stomach did a little flip. Aunt Meg and Maria squealed in unison, dropping the garland they'd been hanging and scrambled to shove the last of the holiday decorations back into boxes. I joined in, helping them clean up the organized chaos just as the car came to a stop.

The three of us gathered by the window, trying not to look like we were spying as a woman finally stepped out of the back seat. She wore a billowing, bright pink dress—almost a muumuu—and a wide-brimmed hat that covered nearly her entire face. From the other side of the car, a second woman emerged, dressed much more casually in jeans and a button-down shirt. Even though I had no real clue what Katherine Kirby looked like in person, it was clear who the star was. The woman in the dress floated above the scene, radiating a diva-like aura, ignoring everything and everyone.

Aunt Meg jolted suddenly, breaking our little trance. "What are we doing standing here, staring?" She smoothed her hair, then hurried to the front door. Maria and I followed close behind, feeling like we were welcoming royalty.

A uniformed driver followed the women up the steps with their luggage. The woman in jeans had shoulder-length brown hair and a mousy nose. She lowered her large sunglasses and stared at the three of us, who were all now standing in the doorway, blocking their entrance.

"Oh, so sorry, come on in," Aunt Meg cried, and we all moved out of the way to let the women inside.

After a moment of awkward jostling, Aunt Meg moved behind the check-in desk near the corner and the woman in jeans approached.

The moment the other one entered, she froze then peered over her shoulder, scanning the room in one long, exaggerated sweep. "Are all the windows secure?" she asked, her voice sharp and dramatic.

I exchanged a glance with Aunt Meg, who looked puzzled but nodded quickly. "Yes, of course. The house is very safe."

She didn't look convinced. "You might want to check them again." She pulled her sunglasses off, revealing striking blue eyes that darted from corner to corner as though she expected someone to leap out from the shadows. "I've had a... situation," she continued, her voice lowering dramatically. "Someone's been following me. A stalker."

Aunt Meg's eyes widened in alarm. "Oh, dear..."

The woman in jeans let out a heavy sigh, clearly fed up. "Katherine, really? Not this again," she muttered under her breath, but loud enough for us all to hear. "You don't have a stalker. You have an imagination."

Katherine shot her a withering look. "I know what I saw, Kelly. He's been watching me. I should've called ahead to see if the theater could beef up security." She glanced out the front window. "Should we call the theater? Is it too late? Maybe we should get someone here..."

I glanced at Aunt Meg, whose pleasant smile faltered just a bit. "Well, we can certainly keep an eye out," she offered gently, though it was clear she wasn't sure how seriously to take the claim. "Maria and I are always around if you need anything."

Katherine ignored her and gave one last suspicious glance at the windows before turning her attention to her phone, now completely ignoring us as if the conversation had never happened.

Kelly shook her head as if she'd had enough drama for a lifetime. "We have a reservation," she said flatly, handing over her ID. "Katherine and Kelly Kirby."

"Of course," Aunt Meg said, working swiftly on the keyboard to pull up their reservation. "You'll be in rooms two and three," she said, grabbing two sets of keys from the wall. Kelly took them with a nod, but Katherine remained near the stairs, wrapped up in some drama on her phone.

"We'll need transportation to the theater in about an hour. I was told there would be transportation available with the rooms?" The woman asked as she scanned the B&B.

Aunt Meg nodded, glancing quickly in my direction and then back to Kelly. "That's right. We're happy to drive you wherever you need to go."

Car service was not a regular deal for guests who stayed at Primrose House, but I figured Aunt Meg had thrown that little perk in to sweeten the deal for the celebrity and convince her to stay with us. I wondered who might get the job of shuttling the women around during their stay.

Aunt Meg handed a sheet of information about the hotel and

area to Kelly and gestured toward Maria. "This is Maria. She'll show you to your room. Please let any one of us know if you need anything during your stay. We have a nightly happy hour and we'll be celebrating Christmas with a few activities throughout the week as well."

Kelly raised an eyebrow. "I'm sure we'll be too busy with theater things."

"Oh, right. Of course. Well, enjoy your stay," Aunt Meg replied with a pleasant smile.

The sisters followed Maria up the stairs, neither of them grabbing their bags, so I quickly moved to their luggage and grabbed one of the heavy cases, foisting it up the stairs behind them. Aunt Meg started to protest, but I gave her a smile. "I've got it! Go ahead and finish up with the decorations!"

Perfume drifted down the stairwell after the women as I followed them to room two.

"What is this, a farmhouse? I thought you were going to find us somewhere decent to stay," Katherine said to her sister as I entered the room and set the bag down. They didn't notice my frown or even my presence.

"Well, it is *Sugar Creek*, sister. What did you expect?"

Katherine whirled and glared at Kelly. "You booked this place to spite me, didn't you? Just another ploy to throw me off my game, no doubt. Fredericksburg has plenty of *decent* hotels."

Kelly sighed, clearly over it. "Not everything's a conspiracy against you, Katherine."

As much as I wanted to be a fly on the wall for their drama, they finally noticed my presence and both stopped talking until I backed out of the room behind Maria. Kelly followed me and shut the door with a thump.

I sighed and headed back down for the rest of their bags. I hoped their attitudes didn't infect everyone else at the B&B. The animosity and coldness were in direct conflict with the holiday cheer I met as I descended and found Aunt Meg dancing to another Christmas jingle as she hung our old stockings over the fireplace.

"I hope those sisters don't bring too much drama with them," I muttered as I grabbed a stocking and hung one too.

Aunt Meg laughed. "It's no problem, honey. I'm sure they'll be fine."

I raised an eyebrow, but she was determined to stay positive, so I let it go.

"I heard them ask for a ride to the theater. I'd be happy to take them over. I need to talk to the manager over there about the party I'm catering, anyway. Now would be a great time," I offered.

"Are you sure? I don't know what I was thinking when I promised them car service, as if we aren't busy enough already!" she said with a laugh.

"It's no problem. I get it. It's a good way to have convinced them to stay. And who knows what kind of publicity we might get with them staying here. It'll certainly be good for Primrose House."

"Well, I appreciate it! I might end up having to ask Ed Morton for his help if things get too crazy around here. Although I know he's busy driving tours around right now, too." Ed owned a local tour bus company, Two-Step Through Texas Tours, and often shuttled B&B guests around.

"I'm happy to help drive as long as I'm not busy with a catering gig. Although, as you know, I've got several of those lined up." My gut did a little lurch at the thought, and a mixture of excitement and fear coursed through me. Finally, after months of barely making it by with my new catering business, Deep in the Heart Catering, the holiday season had kicked in and I was flush with jobs.

"Thank you. I think we'll make it work between you, me, and Maria. And maybe Ed here and there."

I grabbed the rest of the sisters' bags and took them quickly upstairs, putting them next to the closed door before hightailing it back downstairs.

Before Aunt Meg and I could talk anymore, another car pulled into the lot. We watched as a family of four got out of an SUV and started piling luggage onto the ground. "Looks like you've got more guests," I told her as I patted her arm. "I'm going to go finish up those cookie trays, but I can stop anytime if you need me."

She nodded and slid behind the desk to welcome the new arrivals and I headed back to the big old kitchen where I mostly ran my catering business from. Cinnamon and peppermint scented the air and I rolled my shoulders before pulling my apron back on. I surveyed the mess I'd made earlier and tried to figure out what to do next.

One of the many things I'd started to do during the holidays was a drop-off cookie platter service. I'd taken order forms around to businesses and schools, left them at the hair salon and gym, and told everyone I could think of who might want cookies for the holidays that I was providing. I offered a choice between six different specialty cookies and I charged by the half dozen. The program turned out to be more popular than I'd imagined, however, and now I was up to my eyeballs in gingerbread, snicker-doodles, and peppermint twists.

I tested a lemon drop that sat on a cooling rack and decided it was cool enough to add to the half-finished trays nearby. Next, I arranged each one in appetizing rows and then covered the platters with plastic wrap and ribbon and tucked in one of my business cards with a discount offer for catering. There were four platters that needed to be delivered today, but I decided to wait until after I took the sisters to the theater. A broadway diva probably did not want to ride in the same vehicle as a bunch of cookie trays. The thought of it made me laugh, though.

After cleaning up the cookie mess and checking to make sure everything was ready to serve for the happy hour that Primrose House offered every evening, I sat down at the kitchen table for a few minutes and went over my notebook. The holidays would be even more of a balancing act than usual between the cookie platters, the parties I'd been booked to cater, and helping out Aunt Meg where I could with B&B tasks.

One appointment on my calendar caught my eye, and I smiled. My friend Ellie's baby shower was scheduled for Friday evening, the twenty-third. Ellie owned the Sugar Creek Bakery, and she was very pregnant at the moment. Her shower would be a delightful celebration and I was honored that she'd booked me to cater the event. I'd given her a hefty discount as a present, and I planned to go all out to make the event special.

I had several drop-off type parties over the next week leading up to Christmas as well, mostly office holiday parties and small in-home events. But I also had the big theater company party on Christmas Eve after the last performance of the Christmas pageant that starred Katherine Kirby. I knew the annual production, a Christmas medley of acting, singing, and dance, was always a big affair, but with a broadway star gracing us with her performance, I had no doubt it would be a packed house, both for the production and the party. I would need to make much more food than I normally would, but I was already looking forward to making everything special. A theater company on Christmas Eve presented many options, each one funner than the last.

Aunt Meg stuck her head into the kitchen a few minutes later as I was scrolling the internet looking for mini popcorn boxes. "The Kirby sisters are ready to go." She looked at my open notebook and the cookie platters lined up on the counter. "But if you're busy, I can have Maria do it."

"No, no. Now is fine," I told her with a smile. My plans could wait until after my visit to the theater. I closed my notebook and grabbed my phone and purse. If nothing else, I was looking forward to seeing the theater from the inside. I was ashamed to admit I'd never been to the theater myself and I wanted to see if it was like I'd imagined. Getting a good look at the event space would help me decide how to prepare and what to make for the party, too.

The sisters waited at the stairs and Aunt Meg handed me the keys to her sedan as I walked by. "Here, take my car," she told me with a wink.

I smiled and gestured for them to follow, eager to get the show on the road.

CHAPTER TWO

As I grabbed the car and angled it toward the porch to pick the pair up, I bit my lip and eyed the front seat. It could easily hold a few trays of cookies. Would the sisters really mind the smell of sugar permeating their makeshift limousine? Maybe I could drop the cookies off after the theater?

But before I could do something that I might regret, the sisters came down to the car. Kelly was in the same jeans and shirt she'd worn earlier, but Katherine had changed into an all new colorful silky dress. She looked almost like a parrot, the bright greens, pinks, and yellows of the fabric all swirling around her body, making her seem bigger than she actually was. The hat and glasses hadn't changed, though. Those still mostly obscured her face.

"So, you both grew up in Sugar Creek?" I asked as we pulled out onto the main road a minute later.

Kelly frowned and glanced at me through the rearview mirror. Curtly, she nodded. Clearly, they did not want to have a conversation. Which was fine. I would lose myself in my own thoughts of work as we drove the short five minutes to downtown Sugar Creek.

Main Street had been decked out for Christmas since the day

after Thanksgiving, but every time I saw it I got a little jolt of childish holiday excitement. Twinkling lights wrapped around every lamppost and festive displays covered the shop windows. Garlands and red ribbons stretched between buildings, adding to the small-town charm. In Main Street Park, a towering Christmas tree stood proudly, its colorful lights and ornaments in contrast to the crispy dead grass beneath. The town square bustled with activity, children in short sleeves laughing as they rode a small holiday train around the outskirts of the park.

I glanced back at the two sisters, wondering if they noticed the holiday cheer or had any sense of nostalgia for the place where they'd grown up. But their frosty dispositions hinted otherwise. I wondered, could you really perform in a Christmas play if you didn't care about the holiday? Maybe as Scrooge. I realized suddenly that I had no idea what role Katherine was supposed to be playing, or even what the annual play was about. I would likely be working through most of the showings, but I vowed to try to catch one if I could.

As we turned the final corner toward the theater, I noticed how cold the sisters seemed toward each other, too. I'd never had a sister, but I imagined it to be very different from what I saw between these two. Katherine was on her phone, her body shifted away from Kelly and pressed against the door of the car. Kelly gazed out at Sugar Creek with a frown on her face, and her big dark glasses hiding most of her face. Her body, too, was angled away, not toward her sister. Not a peep had passed between them the entire drive.

Pulling up to the curb in front of the small theater, I saw a gaggle of people milling around near the front doors. Katherine let out a deep sigh when she spotted them, but then, like flipping a switch, she pasted on a dazzling smile and stepped out of the car. As soon as the crowd realized it was her, they surged toward us like a wave.

I froze for a second, my stomach tightening as I worried they were going to mob her. Katherine's stalker paranoia bounced around in my head. What if one of them wasn't just a fan?

I jumped out of the car, hurrying to cut off the group before they got too close, but by the time I reached the curb, they'd surprisingly stopped at a respectful distance.

"Miss Kirby!" someone cried, and then her name echoed through the group as they jostled for a better look. There were over a dozen of them—mostly high school-aged kids, though a few local adults were mixed in too. Each one wore a press badge pinned to their jackets.

It felt like overkill to me, but who was I to stop them from taking themselves seriously?

"Kitty, there you are!" A tall, thin man emerged from the theater's front doors a moment later, dressed in trim grey slacks, a burgundy polo, and leather loafers. His hair was thinning at the front, and he made his way quickly toward us, reaching for Katherine's elbow like they were old friends.

She pulled away sharply, casting a wary glance over her shoulder. "It's *Katherine* now, Charles," she corrected him, her voice low and controlled. "No more Kitty, alright?"

Charles blinked, momentarily thrown by her curt response, but he recovered quickly, though there was a tightness in his smile that hadn't been there before. "Of course. My mistake," he said smoothly, though the corners of his eyes crinkled in irritation. "Why don't we head inside? The cast is already on stage, waiting for you." His tone was professional, but a sharp edge of resentment laced his words.

Katherine's gaze lingered on the small crowd, her shoulders stiff as though expecting something—or someone—to lunge out at her. She hesitated just long enough for the "press" to snap a few more photos before turning back to the street to scan the cars like she expected a sniper to be hiding behind one.

Kelly stood off to the side during Katherine's impromptu photo shoot, glued to her phone. She rolled her eyes as Katherine's behavior turned more exaggerated with each passing second. "Katherine, please," Kelly muttered, barely glancing up. "Can you stop acting like we're in a spy thriller for five minutes? No one's after you."

"You don't know that," Katherine hissed, shooting her sister a sharp look. "I have a stalker, Kelly. Just because you don't take it seriously doesn't mean it isn't real."

Kelly snorted and shook her head, still tapping away at her phone. "Right. And I'm sure your stalker's lurking here in Sugar Creek, Texas, population practically zero."

Katherine's lips pressed into a thin line, but she said nothing more. Instead, she threw one more cautious look at the crowd before adjusting her wide-brimmed hat, as if it could shield her from whatever unseen threat she imagined was out there.

Charles, standing a few feet away, shifted uncomfortably. His eyes darted between the sisters, a faint twitch in his jaw as he watched Katherine. "Why don't we get inside," he said, his voice strained. "I'm sure everyone's dying to see you."

The words "dying to see you" had a sharpness to them, but Katherine either didn't notice or chose to ignore it. She gave him a quick, dismissive nod, barely acknowledging him as she started toward the entrance of the theater.

Charles' face tightened as she turned away, the muscles in his jaw flexing as though he were biting back something he desperately wanted to say. I'd never met him before, but in the presence of Katherine, he looked like a man barely holding back years of frustration.

As we moved inside, Kelly was finally pulled from her phone by the theater manager, who greeted her with exaggerated air kisses, his frostiness immediately gone. "Kelly Kirby! You haven't changed a bit!" he gushed.

Kelly smiled and returned the gesture, her tone much lighter now. "Charles, good to see you." But as she followed him inside, I noticed the way her gaze lingered on her sister, almost wary.

I hustled to catch up with the group, figuring that sticking close to the Kirbys was my best shot at finding out who I needed to speak with about the catering. I followed them through the double doors, the bright chatter of the press fading behind us, replaced by the hollow silence of the theater's empty rotunda.

The room was grander than I expected for a small-town theater, with posters of past productions framed along the walls. But what really caught my eye was the enormous sign taking up the center of the floor:

Three Nights Only! The Sugar Creek Christmas Extravaganza featuring local star Katherine "Kitty" Kirby, it proclaimed in bold red and green letters.

I glanced at Katherine, who stood rigid in the center of the room, staring up at the poster of her own face. Her expression was hard to read—was it pride? Or was it anger?

"They'd better get my name right on the playbill," Katherine muttered, more to herself than anyone else. "If they print Kitty again, I'll sue."

Charles, trailing just behind her, barely concealed a scowl. "You know, the town remembers you as Kitty. It's kind of nostalgic, don't you think?"

Katherine turned to him, her expression icy. "Nostalgia doesn't pay the bills, Charles. I'm Katherine now, and I expect to be treated like it."

His smile was thin. "Of course, Katherine." He said her name like it tasted bitter.

She ignored his tone and swept toward the hallway to the right, her wide-brimmed hat tilting just slightly as she glanced at him from the corner of her eye. "Charles, I've had a little issue with a stalker lately. I was hoping we could discuss security..."

Kelly's eyes met mine briefly, and I could see the exhaustion behind her forced smile. "She's always like this," Kelly whispered to me as we trailed behind them. "Dramatic as ever. First, it was someone stealing her costumes, then creepy fan letters, and now this supposed stalker. It never ends."

"Has anyone actually seen this stalker?" I asked quietly.

Kelly raised an eyebrow, but before she could respond, Katherine's sharp voice cut through the silence. "Are you coming or what?" She was already halfway down the hallway, disappearing into a door on the left.

Kelly sighed, shaking her head. "See what I mean?" she muttered before hurrying to catch up with her sister.

As they moved further into the theater, I caught a glimpse of Charles lingering by the door for a moment longer than the others. His eyes were fixed on Katherine's retreating figure, and for just a second, something darker flickered in his expression. But then, just as quickly, he smoothed it away, plastering on the polished theater-manager smile as he followed them into the theater.

Chapter Three

I thought about following them but had a feeling everyone in the performance hall would be too wrapped up in the rehearsal to bother with a caterer, so I decided to poke around outside the main theater area instead.

A couple of ticket booths decorated with pine garlands and red and gold holiday ornaments stood at each side of the entry hall where I stood. Long hallways stretched out in either direction.

As I stood there puzzled, wondering which direction to try, a woman came down the hall toward me and, as soon as she saw me, she frowned. "I'm sorry, miss. But we're closed right now. You'll need to come back when there's a show."

"Oh, I'm not here for a show. I'm the caterer. I was hired for the afterparty on Saturday?"

Her face brightened. "Right! Yes! Okay, come with me, then."

We walked at a brisk pace down the right hallway. It was dim and smelled ancient, but I immediately loved the place. My mind began to play with themed catering ideas in which variations on popcorn featured heavily.

"I'm Abby Hirsch, by the way," I told her as we walked.

She laughed and slowed down. "Sorry, I get a little too far into my own head sometimes. I'm Ruth Goldman," she replied. "I'm one of the Drama Mamas."

I had no idea what a drama mama was, but it must have been an important role. She seemed to know her way around very well and as we passed a couple of people in period costumes, they nodded respectfully to her and she nodded back.

"Okay, this is where we'll do the party," she told me as she swung a heavy door open a moment later.

The room was cavernous, with high ceilings and exposed rafters that gave it an industrial feel. Bright fluorescent lights illuminated a hodgepodge of theatrical paraphernalia scattered throughout the space. Towering set pieces leaned against the walls —the facade of an old house here, a painted backdrop of a forest there. Racks of colorful costumes lined one wall, while shelves stacked with smaller props and oddities filled another. The air was thick with the scent of sawdust and paint, hinting at recent set construction. Despite the clutter, there was a charm to the madness, each piece telling a story of productions past and present. A cleared area in the center of the room, currently occupied by folding tables and chairs stacked in a tumbling mess of metal and plastic, seemed to be the designated space for the upcoming party.

"I'm sure Charles Dunhill will give you all the details. He's the house manager here, so he has the final say in everything theater related. But I know he wants to pull out all the stops. Full bar, plenty of food. Buffet for sure. We want people to feel free to help themselves. Our annual Christmas wrap party is an institution, and especially this year, with Katherine Kirby being here."

Her face lit up with excitement. "Have you met her? I can't believe Charles got such a big star for the production! You know, the two of them used to be friends back in high school. Came up in the drama clubs. Everyone knew them back in the day."

I nodded. "She's staying at my Aunt Meg's B&B, Primrose House. I drove her and her sister over today, will probably do it again too, so I imagine I'll be a regular face around here."

She patted my arm. "Oh, that's lovely, dear. You should sit in on the performance with us sometime, see the nuts and bolts. If you're so inclined."

Just then, another woman came in. "There you are!" she sighed with relief. "I could really use you a minute, Ruth," she told the woman. Ruth glanced at me and I nodded. "Go ahead, I'll just look around and make a few notes, if that's okay."

She nodded and as the women stepped outside, I quickly walked the length of the room to get a feel for how much space I would have to set up a buffet and a bar station. I pulled my notebook out of my purse and made a few notes about the number of chafing dishes and ideas for the bar.

It would be my first time serving alcohol at an event and I was nervous but also excited about it. I'd recently received my liquor license from the city and planned to hire a temporary bartender for the night to man the station. A bar setup would greatly improve my margins and if this event went well, I would happily start offering it as a regular add-on to catering.

The door swung open again, surprising me so much I nearly dropped my pencil, but instead of Ruth, two men walked into the room, deep in conversation with one another.

"I knew it was a bad idea to have her here," one of them said under his breath to the other one as they each picked up a side of a massive wood prop of an old house. "Charles is getting even more crazy than usual."

"I didn't think it was possible, but you're right. He's lost it. Did you hear him screaming about the third act change? It's just small-town theater, dude. Take a chill-pill."

The men walked out of the door awkwardly with the prop. Once the door slammed behind them, I clasped my hands behind my back and paced back and forth across the big space as I waited for Ruth to return. The props once again caught my eye. There must have been enough for half a dozen plays, if not more, and I wondered if they would all still be here for the party or if they planned to clean the room up before then. It was something I needed to ask about, so I knew how much space I would have for the food and beverage stations.

My mind turned to the overheard conversation. They must have been talking about the man who'd taken the sisters in earlier. I wondered what his story was. But before I could wonder too much, the door opened again with a creak.

"Okay! Catering!" Ruth called behind me, breaking my concentration. She came up and squeezed my arm. "Sorry, I got distracted. Easy to do around here. Let's get back to that party."

"I was wondering if these props will all be here during the party, or is the room going to be cleared out?"

Ruth glanced around at the towering hunks of wood and metal around us and laughed. "They're so much a part of things that I forget they're even here sometimes. I doubt they'll be moved. With all the work that still needs to be done for the Christmas play and how stressed out everybody is, finding the muscle to do it probably isn't feasible. Besides, I think the theater crowd likes the ambiance."

I nodded. "That's fine. It's no matter to me. I just need to plan accordingly."

"You'll have to talk to Charles about the rest of the details. I know he'll have a few things to add, but he's very busy right now. Maybe you can come back another time, or he can give you a call?" she suggested. She looked at her watch quickly and I got the hint.

"Okay, that's fine. I appreciate your help."

She nodded and smiled. "Can you find your way out? I need to get back in there," she gestured toward the theater with her thumb, and I nodded.

"Alright, it was nice to meet you, hon. Let any of us Drama Mamas know if you need anything. You'll know us by the pin." She pointed to a hot pink pin on her shirt with "Drama Mamas" written in bold black print.

I stood looking at the hulking props another minute before I followed her out. They were so large and ominous. I didn't really like the look of them, but I would lean into it and try to create an atmosphere of excitement with my catering tables, since I didn't have another choice. It would be a big job, but an exciting one. I couldn't wait to see how I managed.

Chapter Four

As I was leaving the room, I noticed two people in the middle of an argument near the far end of the hallway next to the stage doors. A woman slumped on a bench, her hands balled up in fists at her side and the man stood over her, his hands on his hips and his voice angry. I realized it was the same man who had whisked the sisters away in the front of the theater earlier, Charles. The one I needed to speak with about the party. I debated between waiting for him and trying to call him later. He seemed very angry, so maybe waiting until another time was the right answer.

Their conversation wafted toward me, though, which was surprising given the noise from the direction of the theater and the banging coming from some cavernous space nearby, and I got sucked into eavesdropping despite my best intentions.

Charles hissed, "get it done, now. No more of this garbage, or I'll find someone to replace you so fast your head will spin." He tossed a piece of fabric at the woman's feet and she put her head into her hands.

Charles turned and started to leave, but saw me lingering there. He slowed as he walked by me. "It's so hard to find good help these days…" he muttered before stalking down the hallway. I glanced after him, deciding at once that a discussion of catering could wait for another time.

I knew nothing about the man other than the fact that I didn't like him. Not one bit.

I turned back to the woman who sat on the bench. She was full-on crying now. I rifled through my purse and found a tissue, then went over and handed it to her.

She looked up at me, and my heart went out to her. She was probably in her mid thirties or early forties, with long dark straight hair and wide eyes. Her body was rail thin, almost to the point of being sickly, and the dark circles under her eyes hinted at long nights of work or worry—or both. I wondered what the two had been arguing over. I got the feeling that there was more going on between them than what I'd just witnessed.

"Are you alright?" I asked her.

"I'm sorry," the woman said with a soft nod before blowing her nose. "I shouldn't be so emotional. But he makes me so angry I could scream sometimes, you know?"

I nodded and crossed my arms, torn between leaving her to her emotions and sticking around for her story.

She held her hand out to me, and I shook it. "Lisa Baldwin. I'm the costume designer."

"I'm Abby Hirsch, the caterer," I said with a laugh. Looking at her another moment, I could tell she could use a friendly ear, so I sat down on the bench beside her. My cookie trays could wait a while longer.

"I've worked here for over a decade. Not that it's my only gig, not by a long shot. I do alterations and run a custom Etsy store, too. But that doesn't matter to Charles. He doesn't care about my experience or my dedication to this theater despite the horrible pay. He expects things that are impossible and doesn't believe me when I tell him I can't do it."

She bent and picked up the fabric that sat at her feet and smoothed out the creases.

"Is that for Katherine's costume?" I asked, gesturing to the fabric.

Lisa nodded. "Yes, it's for her finale dress. Charles wants it to be 'spectacular' and 'unforgettable'. But with the budget we have and the time frame..." She shook her head. "Sometimes I think he forgets we're a small-town theater, not Broadway."

"He seemed pretty mean, the way he was talking to you. Is he like that often?"

"Charles can be mean when he's stressed," she said quietly. "This one is much worse than the rest have been, because Katherine Kirby is here. They go way back, or so I've heard. I think he wants to impress her or make her realize how talented he is. Poor Charles has always taken himself too seriously, suffered under the delusion that he's better at this theater thing than he really is. It probably grates at him that an old friend made it on Broadway and he didn't."

I nodded, but didn't say a word. I was totally sucked in and wanted to hear all the juicy gossip about the star and the theater.

"It's hard too that she's just now arrived. We've been practicing this play for over a month already. Everyone's tired and it's tough to suddenly throw her in the mix and have to adjust. But of course, we couldn't expect Miss Kirby to be here for all the rehearsals. I'm sure she wouldn't have wanted to..." her voice trailed off, and the smile faded for a moment before she pasted it back on. "But we're so glad she's here now! The first showing is Thursday night, so we don't have a lot of time for her to get acclimated to the show. But I suppose her being Broadway and all, she'll have no trouble with it," she said with a laugh and a little nervous wave of her hand.

"Hey, Lisa! There you are!" A young woman dressed in a ballet costume came down the hall toward us, her tutu rustling noisily.

Lisa's face lit up. "Abby, this is Brittney. She's been performing in Katherine Kirby's place for our practices."

Brittney gave me a thousand-watt smile and shook my hand. She was absolutely beautiful, probably in her early twenties, with fiery red hair plaited intricately around her head like a crown. Freckles dusted her pale cheeks and nose, giving her a youthful, fresh-faced appearance that contrasted sharply with her graceful dancer's posture. Even standing still, she seemed to vibrate with barely contained energy.

Lisa pointed at me. "She's a caterer. For the Christmas wrap party, I assume?"

I nodded.

"Oh, cool! This is my first year as a performer, but I've heard a lot about those parties. I'm sure it'll be a blast." She turned to Lisa. "Hey, the Drama Mamas are looking for you. Something about Tim's vest?"

She rolled her eyes. "They can wait a few minutes."

I was ashamed to admit to these theater folk that I'd never once set foot inside the Sugar Creek Theater. "The drama mamas?" I asked.

"Yeah, the Drama Mamas are kind of an institution around here. It's a group of women who support the theater and have a lot of sway around here. As far as I know, they started back in the eighties. But over the years they've grown more and more important to the theater," Lisa said.

"It's gotten so bad that you really can't do anything around here anymore without their approval," Brittney said as she glanced around.

She made that sound like a bad thing.

"Why is that?" I asked.

Shrugging, Lisa glanced over my shoulder before answering. "They keep the theater afloat. Without their donations and volunteer work, our little theater would have closed years ago. It's not like this is Broadway or anything. We're lucky if we sell half the tickets for every production we put on. But it gives them a whole lot of say about what goes on around here. What shows we do, who gets what role. That kind of thing."

"But having Katherine here will help with the slow sales, I would imagine," I replied.

"Right. No doubt this year we'll sell out. People all want to see a star," Brittney said with a sigh. "Too bad none of us locals are good enough to get the same kind of attention."

Lisa patted her hand. "You're a fantastic performer, and you know it! You just need a big break. You need someone to come in here and see what you're worth. Or you need to get out of this little town and spread your wings. Who knows, maybe Katherine Kirby will recognize your talent and take you back to Broadway with her."

Brittney rolled her eyes. "Not likely. Have you met her?"

Lisa shook her head. "Not yet. What's she like?"

"She's so self absorbed that I'd be surprised if she even knew anyone else was in this play with her. She is beautiful, though. We'll see how well she can read her lines." Brittney raised her eyebrows and fluffed her tutu. "You're right. What I need to do is go to New York myself. And maybe I just will."

Lisa's face fell at the comment, but she hid it quickly. "Alright, I better go see what's going on with Tim." She stood and turned to me. "Thanks for the Kleenex, and the shoulder to cry on."

I smiled at her. "Anytime. I'm sure I'll see you around."

Brittney nodded and waved to me, and then the two of them headed down the hall and I sat on the bench for another minute, processing everything I'd heard and seen in the last few minutes. It shouldn't have come as a surprise that the theater was such a dramatic place. But I was overwhelmed by all the people and conflicts I'd seen play out in such a short amount of time. Thinking more about the big party, I realized that it would be a good idea to hire some staff to help me this time around. Who knew what craziness might ensue?

As I headed out toward the front, I paused at the doors to the performance hall. Now that I'd met a few people, I felt more comfortable going inside and curiosity got the best of me, so I quietly pushed open one of the heavy doors and stepped in. The theater was dimly lit, with most of the illumination coming from the bright stage lights. The room smelled of old velvet seats and wooden floorboards, a scent that spoke of countless performances and years of history.

On stage, a group of actors were running through a scene, their voices echoing in the cavernous space. I could make out Brittney among them, her graceful movements eye-catching next to the more stilted actions of some of the other performers.

In the front row, I noticed a tight-knit group of women I assumed were the Drama Mamas. They sat with perfect posture, occasionally whispering to each other and making notes in small notebooks, an air of authority around them.

Charles was pacing back and forth in the aisle, his brow furrowed in concentration. Every so often, he would stop to bark out a direction or criticism to the actors on stage. The director, a thin man with wild gray hair, stood nearby, gesticulating wildly as he tried to explain something to a confused-looking actor.

Off to the side, I spotted Kelly sitting alone, furiously typing on her phone. Her face was set in a scowl, and she seemed oblivious to the activity around her. I guessed this was old-hat for her. It made me wonder what role she played in her sister's career. It must be something important, given how closely she followed Katherine around. I wondered if they ever got tired of being so joined at the hip.

I glanced around another minute before heading back out the theater door. The last thing I needed was to get pulled into another conversation. I'd already been here longer than planned and I had plenty of catering work on my plate.

When I stepped outside, the bright afternoon sun shocked me after the dim theater and I squinted and rooted around in my purse for my sunglasses. A couple of the high school reporters milled about near the theater doors as I left. They had a momentary jolt of excitement followed by disinterest and disappointment as they realized I wasn't Katherine Kirby. I grinned at them and they turned back to their phones, unimpressed.

As I headed toward Aunt Meg's car, my mind drifted back to the catering work waiting for me. The theater party was shaping up to be a much bigger production than I'd anticipated, and with the Drama Mamas hovering like hawks, I needed to be on my game. I definitely needed to hire some help.

But first, I needed to get some cookie trays delivered.

Chapter Five

Sugar Creek was blessedly small, so the cookie deliveries only took a quarter of an hour once I finally got the trays all loaded in my catering van back at Primrose House. I was only asked about Katherine Kirby at one stop, which surprised me, given the gossip network in town. I would've thought a major star staying at the B&B would get people talking, but I was pleasantly surprised. Either word hadn't gotten out about her visit—except to those junior reporters that had dogged us at the theater—or people didn't realize where she was staying or who I was in relation to Aunt Meg.

The lack of interest was a blessing for me, though. It meant my errands finished up earlier than expected and as I drove back through Main Street, I got an idea. I pulled up a minute later in front of the Sugar Creek Police Department to visit my boyfriend, Sheriff Ryan Iverson.

As I pushed open the heavy glass door of the station, I was immediately enveloped by warmth and the scent of cinnamon. The lobby dripped with garlands, twinkling lights, little stockings, and a small Christmas tree in the corner. I smiled, knowing the decorations were likely the work of someone other than the officers themselves.

"Well, hello there, Abby!" a cheerful voice called out. I turned to see Irene, the new dispatcher, beaming at me from behind her desk. She was a plump, middle-aged woman with kind eyes and salt-and-pepper hair that frizzed around her face. Glasses drooped on her nose as her fingers pushed a needle back and forth at lightning speed on her latest cross-stitch project.

"Hi, Irene," I replied, approaching her desk. "The place looks great! Did you do all this?"

Irene's eyes twinkled. "Sure did! These boys wouldn't know the first thing about making a place feel festive. I just love Christmas, don't you?"

I nodded, admiring the intricate design she was stitching. "Is that a new project?"

"Oh, this?" She held up the hoop. "Just a little something for my granddaughter. Now, what brings you by? Looking for that handsome sheriff of yours?"

Before I could answer, Ty Clayburn, Cassie's fiancé and Sugar Creek deputy, emerged from the back office. "Hey, Abby! Fancy seeing you here," he said with a grin.

"Hey, Ty," I replied, giving him a quick hug. "Just thought I'd drop by and say hi to Ryan. Is he around?"

Ty nodded. "Yeah, I think he's just wrapping up some paperwork. Should be out in a minute. Y'all set for Christmas over at the B&B? I heard you had some exciting guests staying this year."

I grinned and leaned my elbows on Irene's desk. "We do! A broadway star, Katherine Kirby, and her sister, Kelly. I guess they were locals here back when they were kids. I took them over to the theater today, woo! It's crazy over there."

Irene's eyes were wide and excited. "I love the theater. That Christmas production should be something else. I can't wait. I've got tickets for opening night. And I heard about Katherine Kirby, my friend Blanche had a daughter in her grade. I think they were friends, even. What's she like? I've never met anyone famous before."

I shrugged. "I didn't get much of a chance to talk with her," I said, thinking back to how cold she'd been. "She seems...like a celebrity," I said with a small laugh.

Our conversation was interrupted when Ryan came down the hall, a coffee cup in hand and his hair standing up every which way. He saw me and blushed, then moved a hand over his head, trying to sort himself out.

But there was no need. He was gorgeous, no matter how messy his hair was. Strong jaw quirked into a smile, ruddy cheeks, and broad shoulders that stretched his sheriff's uniform. I thought I could look at him for the rest of my life and not get tired of the view.

"I just wanted to stop by and say hi," I said, smiling as he approached. He leaned over and kissed me on the lips and I felt a tingle of desire course through my body.

Pulling away, he rubbed the small of my back. "I'm glad you did. Things were getting a little stale around here. Am I right, y'all?" He said as he glanced at Ty and Irene. They both nodded. "Nice to have a surprise now and again. Breaks up the drudgery of paperwork."

I laughed and leaned into him. "Well, I'm glad I stopped, then."

Ryan glanced at his watch, then back at me with a twinkle in his eye. "You know, I'm just about done here. Have you got time for dinner? We could head over to Lulu's and grab some barbecue if you're feeling up to it."

The thought of Lulu's famous brisket made my stomach rumble. I realized I hadn't eaten since my hurried lunch hours ago. "That sounds perfect, actually. I'm starving."

"Great," Ryan said, his face lighting up. He turned to Ty. "You good to hold down the fort?"

Ty waved us off. "Go on, get out of here. Irene and I've got everything under control."

"Just give me a minute and I'll wrap a few things up," he told me as he headed back down the hall to his office. While I waited for him, Irene and I talked about Christmas plans and she told me all about her daughter, who was off at college and constantly in trouble of some kind or other. I laughed and consoled her in equal measure and thought to myself that if I had any extra time, it might be nice to make up some cookie trays and take them around to Sugar Creek families like Irene's on Christmas Eve.

We said our goodbyes and stepped out into the crisp evening air. Despite the lack of snow, the weather was delightfully cool after the sun went down and I leaned into Ryan for warmth. Main Street was aglow with twinkling lights strung between the lampposts, casting a warm, festive glow over the sidewalks. Wreaths adorned shop doors, and the scent of pine and cinnamon drifted from the candle store on the corner.

As we strolled hand in hand down the street, the stress of the day seemed to melt away. Couples and families were out enjoying the evening, ducking in and out of stores or heading to dinner like us. We passed Mr. Johnson sweeping the sidewalk in front of his hardware store, and he tipped his hat to us with a friendly smile.

"It's been nice and quiet the last few weeks and we're hoping it'll continue through the holidays. Ty's planning to head over to Dallas for a few days for Christmas and I would love it if I could take it easy for a spell, too. Crossing my fingers, but we haven't had any major incidents for a few weeks now."

I nodded. Cassie had told me all about the Dallas plans. It would be her first time meeting Ty's extended family and now that they were engaged, she had a lot more nerves about being around his family than she had in the past.

"You're still planning on coming over to the B&B for Christmas dinner, right?"

"Of course," he replied, leaning in and grabbing me for a quick squeeze. "I wouldn't miss your cooking for anything!"

We laughed, and I grabbed his hand and squeezed. "Good answer, mister."

As we approached Lulu's, the savory smell of smoked meat filled the air, making my mouth water. The warm glow from the restaurant's windows was inviting, and I couldn't think of a better way to end my busy day than sharing a meal with Ryan.

Stepping inside, the warmth enveloped us like a cozy blanket. Festive garlands and twinkling lights adorned the wooden beams overhead, and a small Christmas tree stood in the corner, decorated with miniature cowboy boots and lassos. I loved that even here, in the no frills local barbecue joint, Christmas was in the air.

We made our way to the counter, where a chalkboard menu hung above, decorated with hand-drawn holly leaves. Ryan nudged me gently. "What're you in the mood for? The pulled pork sandwich is calling my name."

I scanned the menu, my mouth watering. "I think I'll go for the brisket. Oh, and we have to try the sweet potato fries."

After placing our order, we found a cozy booth near the window. Someone had tucked a sprig of mistletoe into the ribbon of the small candle in a mason jar that flickered between us. Ryan saw it and smiled. "I think you owe me a kiss."

I blushed and shook my head, biting my lip. "Only if it's hanging over our heads, right?"

He grabbed the candle from the bottom and held it over his head. "Come here, you."

Pushing up on my elbows, I leaned over the table and our lips met for a long soft kiss that probably lasted a beat too long given that we were in a public restaurant. But as much as I felt eyes on us, I wanted even more to feel Ryan's lips on mine, so I leaned in a beat longer before pulling away.

Ryan grinned as he set the candle down, his eyes sparkling. After a long minute of us staring at each other like lovesick teens, Ryan cleared his throat. "I bet Cassie's thrilled to have you back at her place. How's that been going? You two still binge-watching every murder mystery show in existence?"

I laughed as I sat back in the booth. "Oh yeah, she couldn't wait to get me back in the guest room, especially with the holidays coming up. Between her estate sale hauls and my catering business, we've basically turned her house into a warehouse."

Ryan grinned, leaning back in his chair. "Sounds cozy, though."

I smiled, but the thought lingered a bit longer than I wanted. "It is, but I'm going to have to figure out something soon. With the wedding coming in the spring... well, I can't exactly keep living with them." I tried to sound casual, but the reality of it weighed on me more than I'd expected.

Ryan's expression softened as he leaned forward, his hand brushing against mine. "You've got some time, but I know it's been on your mind."

I shrugged, knowing he was right, but also not willing to give up my anxiety about the impending life change.

"Speaking of weddings...how are the wedding plans coming along? Cassie driving you crazy yet?" He asked.

I laughed, shaking my head. "You have no idea. Yesterday, she changed her mind about the centerpieces for the third time this week. I love her, but all this fuss is exactly why I've decided that if I ever get married, it'll be a quick trip to the justice of the peace."

Ryan raised an eyebrow. "Oh really? No dream wedding for Abby Hirsch?"

"Nope," I said firmly. "Give me a simple ceremony and a good meal with friends and family any day. All this planning is making me appreciate simplicity even more than I did before."

Ryan chuckled. "I can see that. Though I have to admit, part of me would love to see you all dolled up in a fancy wedding dress."

I felt my cheeks warm at the thought, suddenly realizing that Ryan and I were having a conversation about my eventual wedding. A tiny flicker of a thought passed through my mind—

would it be to him? It caught me off guard and I was silent a moment too long. Ryan noticed and grabbed my hand, rubbing his thumb along mine. I wondered if he'd had the same thought, but before either of us got too carried away, our food arrived.

We tucked into the delicious food but my mind stayed on Ryan and weddings. After a minute, I took a drink of my tea and said, "well, maybe I'd make an exception for the dress. But only if I can wear cowboy boots underneath."

Ryan laughed, his eyes sparkling. "It wouldn't surprise me one bit."

As we turned our attention back to dinner, I couldn't shake the lingering warmth from our conversation. Cowboy boots under a wedding dress... with Ryan by my side? I pushed the thought away, although reluctantly, and focused my attention on the delicious meal and the handsome company.

As we finished eating, our conversation drifted to lighter topics. We chatted about the upcoming Christmas festivities at the B&B, Ryan's hopes for a quiet holiday season at the station, and my ambitious plans for holiday catering. The warm glow of the restaurant and Ryan's company had melted away the day's stress, leaving me feeling content and festive.

Before we knew it, the restaurant was preparing to close. We reluctantly left our cozy booth, stepping back out into the crisp night air. Ryan walked me to the car, his arm wrapped protectively around my shoulders. With a gentle kiss goodnight and promises to talk tomorrow, we said our goodbyes. As I watched him walk back into the station, I couldn't help but feel a flutter of excitement for what the future might hold for us.

CHAPTER SIX

The next morning I got to Aunt Meg's house after stopping for a grocery run and I found the place much quieter than I'd expected. Christmas music played softly in the background and the front room was tidy but nobody was around. Carrying an armful of groceries into the kitchen, I found Aunt Meg and Maria both huddled over a cookbook.

"Ah ha! Just who we needed!"

I raised an eyebrow and set my heavy load on the counter. "What are you two up to?"

"I was thinking about doing something a little bit special for happy hour tonight. We have another couple arriving today and I thought we could do a fire in the fireplace and make something special. I was looking for a homemade eggnog recipe, something that would be good for the kids, but also the adults, if they want to put rum or something in theirs. Do you even put rum into eggnog? These are the questions we have, and we're desperate for a professional!" She put her hand to her forehead and leaned back like she was going to faint.

Looking over my shoulder, I laughed and said, "you've been hanging out with Katherine Kirby too much, I believe."

Maria laughed and Aunt Meg pretended to pout. "What, I could be in the theater if I wanted!"

Maria and I exchanged a look and nodded as we laughed, knowing Aunt Meg would never have the patience for such a thing. Putting the groceries away, I glanced over at their cookbook and realized it was one of those old plastic binder sort of things from the Junior League or some such. "Let me see that," I said as I grabbed it and leafed through a minute, then made a face when I happened upon a recipe for Jellied Veal Ring.

"Why are you looking at this thing? Nobody could cook in the seventies! This kind of thing should be banned from public consumption! You need the internet!"

I finished putting the groceries away and then motioned for them to follow. The three of us headed into the front room to poke around on the computer for recipes. It surprised me to realize that I had no idea how eggnog was made either, or what alcohol would work well with it. But as we did some searching, it gave me an idea, and I suddenly decided to come up with my own special eggnog recipe for the theater wrap party. It would be perfect since there was a mixed crowd of adults and underage people. Although, as soon as I thought it I realized I'd have to check in with the bartender I'd hired to make sure he was strict about not serving alcohol to minors.

We found a recipe, and I helped them make the eggnog before turning back to my own chores. I moved quickly as I gathered eggs, milk, heavy cream, sugar, and nutmeg and Aunt Meg found a pot. I separated the eggs, whipping the whites into soft peaks while Aunt Meg beat the yolks with sugar until they were pale and creamy. Maria warmed the milk and cream in a saucepan, carefully tempering the egg mixture before combining everything on low heat. We took turns stirring the mixture as it thickened, filling the kitchen with a rich, spicy aroma and I couldn't help but dance around to the Christmas music that made its way into the kitchen from the front room. Aunt Meg and Maria smiled when they saw me and started to dance around the kitchen, too.

After the eggnog had cooled, we added a splash of vanilla and a generous dusting of freshly grated nutmeg. The result was a smooth, velvety drink that was worlds apart from the store-bought version. I was pleasantly surprised at how good the homemade drink was and although I had a few ideas about how to change the recipe; it was very close to what I wanted to use for the party.

"Not too shabby," Aunt Meg said as she tasted it. Maria nodded in agreement. "Thanks for saving us from ourselves, Abby girl," she said with a laugh.

I grinned as I started to sort through ingredients for my prep work. "No problem, happy to help. You really should throw that thing out, you know," I said, pointing a chef's knife at the offensive vintage cookbook.

Aunt Meg looked wounded. "Absolutely not! Bertie gave me that in high school!"

I held up my hands with another laugh. "Never mind, then! How silly of me!"

Once we were done with the eggnog and Aunt Meg and Maria had moved on to other B&B tasks, I turned to the rest of my prep duties. The first of my scheduled parties would be a drop off affair tomorrow at lunchtime. I busied myself getting ingredients for sandwich trays and cheese boards out and working. But before long, Aunt Meg came back into the kitchen with a dour look on her face.

"The sisters are asking for a ride to the theater. I can do it if you plan to stick around, but Maria's out running errands, so I don't want to leave the B&B alone if you plan on going somewhere. I can call Ed and see if he's free..."

I waved a hand. "No, I can take them. I actually need to go back to the store, anyway. We're almost out of butter, and I forgot this morning."

Her face turned to shock. "Not the butter! Can't do Christmas without the butter!"

I laughed and nodded. "True, true. Okay, give me five minutes to finish this up and I'll drive them over."

I quickly packed up the trays I was working on and popped them into the fridge, then I sent a quick email to the staffing service I used for occasional part time help to ask for an extra server for Saturday night before once again taking Aunt Meg's keys and heading out to the lot to pull her car around in my new role as chauffeur.

The sisters were just as disinterested in each other as they had been the day before, although I noticed that today Katherine was staring out the window at the town passing by rather than hiding in her phone. I wondered if she was keeping an eye out for the stalker she kept mentioning, or simply lost in nostalgic thought. It got me thinking again about what she must have been like in high school. Had she been popular or an outcast? Had she liked her time here in Sugar Creek or loathed it?

She caught me staring at her through the rearview mirror and glared at me a second before turning back to her phone, shutting down any hint of possibility of asking her the questions that swirled in my mind.

"You remember how Mama used to take us over to the Dairy Queen sometimes?" Katherine asked Kelly all of a sudden.

I glanced back and saw that Kelly was still staring at her phone, but her fingers had come to a complete stop. "Yeah, I remember you always getting a double scoop. Little miss star."

"That was on the good days," Katherine said low, still looking out at the passing town. "On bad days, I got double whoopins."

Kelly glanced at her sideways and turned back to her phone. "It was bad for me too, you know. Just forget all that. It was a long time ago. See, this is why we shouldn't have come back here."

Katherine shrugged, and the sisters fell silent again until we got to the theater. It was an incredibly intimate glimpse into their lives, and I was surprised they'd let their guard down around me. Then again, they were probably so used to help around that they barely even noticed my presence. The sadness in both of their voices, and the hurt, stuck with me as I pulled up to the theater. I knew next to nothing about them, but it sounded like they'd had a difficult childhood.

As I parked near the front, we were greeted by another crowd of local paparazzi, if that's what you could call the ragtag group. But today the group had thinned considerably. Evidently, their lack of success at getting a candid interview the day before had discouraged a good portion of them. I couldn't say I blamed them, although they would probably need to dig deep and find some perseverance if they planned to make it in the news industry.

Katherine and Kelly had no trouble brushing past the weak cries for interviews as they headed straight inside. I hesitated on the curb next to the car. Should I go in and try to talk to Charles about the party or leave it for another time? After what I'd seen of him the day before, I wasn't in much of a rush to see him again. Maybe a call would be best.

But at the last second, I changed my mind and quickly locked up the car before heading into the theater, too. I wanted to poke around some more, take another look at the party room. And if I was honest, eavesdrop on more drama. I didn't have all day though, so I had to be quick about it, and then get back to cooking.

A great pounding racket came from the doors leading into the theater, but instead of heading in that direction I meandered down the right hall, back toward the prop room that would host the party on Saturday night. A few stage hands and actors passed me, most of them ignoring me but a few nodding. No one I recognized.

I came to the door that led to the party space and stuck my head inside but the lights were off and I didn't want to make a nuisance of myself so after glancing around the dim crowded space I shrugged and headed back toward the front of the place.

But as I was leaving, I grew curious about what was at the other end of the hall, the one I hadn't seen the day before, and so I took a minute to wander in that direction as well. The very first door I came across had "House Manager" printed on it and my eyes lit up. Maybe Charles was in his office and I could get a head-count and finalize the menu for the party. But after I knocked and stood there a good long while and then knocked a second time, I still got no answer so I pulled out one of my cards and scrawled on the back, "call me about the wrap party please!" and stuck it under the door.

I straightened and frowned, wondering if there was any other way to get a final headcount. My logical brain told me this detail could wait, but the frantic planner that controlled everything I did demanded an answer.

For now, I would have to let that side of myself wonder. I needed to get to the store for butter and then back to the kitchen to put more cookie boxes together before it got too late, so I started to head toward the front door. But suddenly a scream rang out from a room at the other end of the hall and my heart rate immediately skyrocketed as I moved in the direction it had come from.

"Help!" came a woman's voice again, and I started to run.

Chapter Seven

A group of people had gathered near a door by the time I got to where the scream seemed to have come from. As soon as I stopped at the door, I found it open and Charles standing in the doorway blocking the view, his hands to his mouth, shaking his head.

I pushed him gently aside and found a horrible sight. Katherine Kirby was spread out on a couch by the far wall. She looked dazed and sick and clearly she had thrown up recently. The room stank of it.

But Kelly Kirby was lying on the floor, facedown, and somehow I guessed from the instant I saw the way she was angled that she was dead.

People pushed up against me, trying to get a look, and suddenly my mind snapped to attention. I thought, *what would Ryan want to happen right now*? I knew the answer instantly, so despite the shock and the confusion and the sadness that I felt, I straightened my shoulders and in a loud voice said, "Okay, everyone, step back! Is anyone a doctor or have medical training?" I glanced again at Katherine. She was pale and her eyes were shut, but she was alive, unlike her sister.

Unfortunately, no one stepped forward and even as I waited in vain for an answer, I dialed 911. Quickly I told the dispatcher what had happened, that we needed an ambulance right away. When I hung up the phone, I stuck my head back inside the dressing room as I bit my lip. Katherine was moaning over on the couch, clutching her stomach, and I was torn between going to her and trying to help her and staying out of what was very likely a crime scene.

As much as I wished I could have done something to help the woman, though, I had no medical training whatsoever. I knew there was nothing I could do that was worth going inside that dressing room. So I focused on keeping people out of the room and trying to calm everyone down.

"Help is on the way," I told the crowd. "Who found them?"

"I... I did," an older woman said, her voice shaky. She wore one of the Drama Mama pins and her hands were shaking as she talked. "I was walking past the dressing room when I heard someone cry out for help. It sounded urgent, so I rushed in." She paused, taking a deep breath before continuing. "What I saw was... awful. Both Katherine and Kelly were on the floor. Katherine was conscious but very pale, and Kelly... she wasn't moving at all."

The woman's eyes darted around nervously and landed on Charles before she added, "There was a champagne bottle knocked over beside them. I helped Katherine to the couch—she could barely stand. I was about to check on Kelly when Charles burst in. He took one look at the scene and practically shoved me out of the room, saying he'd handle it."

Charles glared at her, his arms folded over his chest. "I didn't push you, Madeline. Let's not be dramatic," he muttered. "I wanted to make sure she was all right, that's all."

"Well, it felt like a shove to me," she shot back. Ruth rubbed her back in sympathy.

Three EMTs arrived before the argument could continue. They moved through the crowd with neat efficiency and I pointed them to the door where the women were. They all entered the dressing room before shutting the door behind them. As much as I wanted to see what was going on, it was a smart move. The crowd was hungry for the unfolding drama and I knew if they were allowed to watch, it would turn into a major spectacle. As soon as that door closed, everyone backed up and began talking to each other excitedly.

"Can you believe this? It's going to go viral," one of the high school boys said near me. He and a group of performers and stage hands gathered around his phone. I leaned over to see that he'd recorded some of what had happened—including me bossing the crowd around—and had already posted it on social media.

"Hey, you shouldn't do that!" I told him and tried to angle toward his phone. Not that I had any authority with these people, but it seemed so wrong.

He gave me a sour look and moved away. "Get real, lady. This is public property. I can film anything I want."

Before I could try to interfere anymore with the hooligan, Ryan strode down the hallway toward me, Ty and another deputy right behind him. His presence was so striking in his sheriff's uniform, and he was so very much in charge, that every person in the hall quieted.

He noticed me in the crowd and moved quickly to my side, squeezing my arm affectionately before leaning in. "Abby, hey, what's going on?"

I told him quietly about the sisters inside, how it looked to me like they'd been poisoned, but I hadn't gotten a good enough look to know for sure. He glanced at the group of theater people around him and nodded. Surveying the crowd, he set his jaw and asked Ty, "can you secure this area? Start getting statements?"

Ty nodded, and Ryan and the other deputy stepped inside the dressing room before shutting the door again.

Ty glanced around at the crowd. His energy was different from Ryan's. Still in control, still powerful, but I didn't feel the same intensity that I had from Ryan. That could just be more hormones reacting to the man I was in love with, though, I mused.

"Alright, folks, I'll need statements from you all and your contact information as well. If you'll just stick around until I get to you, I'd appreciate it."

There were grumbles, but everyone stayed put. A few in the group rushed toward him, trying to give him their stories first, either because they wanted to get the heck out of dodge or because they had something juicy to share.

He turned to me before he started with the others and said quietly, "I'd like to get your story, too, but if you need to go, I can get your statement later."

I shook my head. "No, I can stay for a while. I drove the sisters here, anyway, so if Katherine is okay, I'll probably drive her back to Primrose House." Although, thinking back to her pallor, I doubted she would be going back to the B&B with me. Still, I wanted to stick around, if for no other reason than to find out what happened and overhear what everyone had to say about what they saw.

I stood close enough to Ty that I could eavesdrop. As much as I knew that Ryan and Ty didn't need my help with this situation, I couldn't shake my own unquenchable curiosity. I wanted to know just as bad as everyone else what had happened to the star and her sister. If Ty realized what I was doing, he didn't acknowledge it, so I clung to the wall and listened to what the theater people had to say. Much of it was speculation and wild exaggeration, and I started to tune out after the third teenager began her tale.

My attention was drawn instead to a hushed but animated conversation among the Drama Mamas who stood nearby. They were huddled together, their voices low but intense. I inched closer, straining to hear.

"This is a disaster," Ruth hissed, her eyes darting around. "Opening night is in two days. What are we going to do?"

Another woman shook her head. "We can't possibly go on with the show now. It would be in poor taste."

"Poor taste?" A third woman scoffed. "This is the most publicity Sugar Creek Theater has had in years. We'd be fools not to capitalize on it."

Ruth gasped. "Barbara! A woman might be dead."

"And that's tragic," Barbara replied, not sounding particularly upset. "But think about it. 'Broadway star's sister dies mysteriously on opening week.' People will be clamoring for tickets."

The other woman nodded slowly. "She has a point. But what about Katherine? She's in no state to perform."

"That's where Brittney comes in," Barbara said, a sly smile spreading across her face. "She's been understudying the role for over a month. This could be her big break. And wouldn't that be a good thing? You know that girl's got talent. Maybe she'd remember us, unlike Kitty, who clearly forgot where she came from and who she owes for the success she has."

"I don't know," Ruth said, biting her lip. "It seems wrong somehow."

"Wrong?" Barbara's voice rose slightly before she caught herself and lowered it again. "What's wrong is letting this theater go under after all we've done for it. This is our chance to put Sugar Creek on the map."

As they continued debating, I felt a chill run down my spine. Their callousness shocked me. A woman had probably just died, and all they could think about was ticket sales and publicity. I glanced at Ty, wondering if he had overheard any of this, but he was focused on interviewing another nervous-looking teenager, this one in a Dickens style costume.

I turned back to the Drama Mamas just in time to hear Ruth say, "Well, I suppose what's done is done. We should talk to Charles about making an announcement..."

Their voices faded as they moved away, heads still bent together in whispers. I stood there, stunned by what I'd heard. It seemed the Drama Mamas were more concerned with the show's success than with Kelly's potential death. Could ambition for the theater have driven one of them to do something drastic? I doubted it, but I would tell Ryan about the overheard conversation and see what he thought.

As Ty finished with the stagehand and moved on to his next interview, I made a mental note to keep a close eye on the Drama Mamas. Something told me there was more to their story than met the eye.

After a few more minutes of listening to Ty interview people without learning anything new, the dressing room door finally opened and a couple of EMTs moved quickly out to the front of the theater and returned a minute later carrying two stretchers. All of us grew quiet and waited for them to move Katherine and Kelly, and it didn't take long. Only a moment later, two of them came out carrying Katherine on one of the stretchers. She was very pale still and her eyes were glassy, but she waved at the group of us weakly and muttered, "the show must go on," as they carried her quickly out of the theater.

It was a strange thing to say, given what was transpiring. I wondered if she was aware of what had happened with her sister or if she was in her right mind at all.

Another few mostly silent minutes passed before a second set of EMTs came out the door with a second stretcher between them, but this one was covered with a sheet.

My theory was confirmed: Kelly Kirby was dead.

CHAPTER EIGHT

After the sisters were taken away and Ty had gotten most everyone's statements the crowd thinned considerably. The drama and excitement of the moment had moved on. I wondered about the boy who'd posted the video of what had happened, what kind of chaos that act would create, and whether there would be any consequences. He'd disappeared with his friends while I'd been concentrating on eavesdropping and I'd never gotten another chance to try to get him to delete the video.

Not that it was my job to do that, anyway. It just felt like such an unsympathetic thing to do, to post someone's suffering for entertainment purposes. I wondered too about the legality of it all, especially now that it was clear that Kelly was dead. But I hadn't really seen what was on the video and I was no lawyer, so I tried hard to push the problem out of my mind. What could I do about it, anyway, other than to tell Ryan, which I would? Let the authorities deal with it.

And right as I thought it, Ryan finally stepped out of Katherine's dressing room. He started to move in my direction, but then noticed Ty talking to Brittney, the actor I'd met the day before. He gave me a quick wave and then moved over to listen to their conversation.

I drifted closer as Ryan moved beside Ty, my curiosity getting the better of me. The faint smell of greasepaint and dust that had permeated the air before the horrible event in the dressing room was now tinged with something more acrid—perhaps the lingering scent of fear and shock.

"... and how long have you been rehearsing Katherine's role?" Ty was asking.

Brittney straightened her shoulders. "Since the beginning of production. About six weeks now."

"That's a long time to prepare for someone else's part," Ryan commented. "How did you land this opportunity?"

A fleeting look of frustration crossed Brittney's face before she composed herself. "I auditioned, like everyone else. I've been working really hard to get the part just right."

From nearby, I overheard one of the older cast members mutter to another, "Auditioned? Please. Charles had her pegged for the role before she even opened her mouth."

Brittney's eyes darted towards the whispers, a slight flush creeping up her neck. "I mean, yes, I auditioned, but Mr. Dunhill did say I was the right person..."

"And how do you feel about Ms. Kirby taking over the role now?" Ty asked, his tone neutral.

Brittney's smile tightened almost imperceptibly. "Oh, it's... it's an honor, really. To work with someone of her caliber. I'm just grateful for the experience."

Despite her attempt at composure, I noticed her fingers fidgeting with the hem of her shirt, a nervous habit that didn't match her calm exterior. Her eyes, wide and expressive, kept darting between Ryan, Ty, and the end of the hallway where Charles had disappeared earlier.

There was something in her demeanor that struck me as odd. While she spoke about the honor of working with Katherine, her tone lacked the enthusiasm I would have expected from having met someone with such a star quality who might help her find her way or act as a mentor. Instead, there was an undercurrent of... was it resentment? Frustration? I couldn't quite put my finger on it, but it was clear that Brittney's feelings about the situation were more complicated than she was letting on. Although, having met Katherine myself, this wasn't overly surprising. I doubted the star had given Brittney the time of day.

As Ryan opened his mouth to ask another question, I saw Charles appear at the far end of the hallway. He caught Brittney's eye, giving her a stern look. Brittney suddenly straightened.

"I'm sorry, but I really need to get going," she said. "I don't know anything else that could be helpful, really. May I please leave?"

Ryan frowned but nodded, his gaze lingering on Charles for a moment before turning to Ty and whispering to him for a moment. Ty nodded and closed his notebook, then headed into the dressing room, giving me a quick smile as he passed.

As Brittney hurried away, Ryan's shoulders slumped slightly, the weight of the investigation clearly bearing down on him. His eyes scanned the hallway, and when they landed on me again, his gaze softened. For a moment, I saw past the professional facade to the man I was falling for and my heart bounced around in my chest.

Ryan made his way over to me, navigating around the few remaining onlookers. As he approached, I could see the conflict in his eyes—the desire to reach out and comfort me warring with the need to maintain a professional distance.

"Hey," he said softly, his voice a mixture of warmth and concern. He glanced around quickly, then reached out and gave my hand a gentle squeeze. The brief contact sent a flutter through my chest.

"You holding up okay?" he asked, his eyes searching mine.

I nodded, trying to put on a brave face. "I'm fine. Just... processing everything."

Ryan's gaze lingered on me for a moment longer, and I could see he wanted to say more, to offer more comfort. Instead, he took a deep breath, shifting back into sheriff mode.

"You were the one who found them?" he asked, his tone becoming more professional, though I could still hear the underlying concern.

I shook my head, feeling the weight of his hand as it reluctantly slipped away from mine.. "No, but I came as soon as I heard the scream. One of the Drama Mamas found them. I saw what was going on and got everyone out of the room as fast as I could, then called y'all."

"Drama Mamas?"

"It's a group of women who seem to be fixtures around here. Sounds like they fund a lot, are here often. They would be a good group to talk to." I thought back to what I'd heard them saying earlier and wondered again if one of them had the nerve to have attempted...and carried out... murder.

He nodded. "Who else was in the room when you got here?"

I thought back to the chaotic scene. "The house manager, Charles. He was standing in the doorway when I arrived, but I don't know what role he had to play in everything. What do *you* think happened?"

Ryan glanced around again and leaned in, even though we were mostly alone. "It looks like they were poisoned, but we'll need to do all the usual legwork before we know for sure. Did you see anything else that might be important?"

I closed my eyes for a moment, going back over the scene. Unfortunately, though, I was so shocked by the state of both sisters that I'd barely noticed anything. I frowned. "Not really. Just that Kelly seemed to be dead. She was on her back. And Katherine was sick on the couch. The room smelled bad."

"Okay. That's alright. They're staying with y'all at the B&B?"

I nodded. "Yeah, and there's something you should know about Katherine," I added, lowering my voice. Ryan's eyes flickered with interest, and I continued, "She kept talking about having a stalker. I don't know how serious it is—or even if it's true. Kelly didn't seem to believe it, and honestly, I couldn't tell if Katherine was being dramatic or if there was something to it."

Ryan frowned, taking in the information. "Did she give you any details?"

"Not much. She was pretty vague, just saying someone had been following her. I don't think she told anyone else, at least not at the theater. She was paranoid, though, checking windows, asking Aunt Meg about security at the B&B. It could be nothing, but I thought you should know."

He nodded, deep in thought. "Thanks. I'll look into it. Might be worth talking to her once she's stable. Could be unrelated, or it could be the key to all this."

"Yeah," I said, wondering myself if Katherine's claims were just another piece of the Kirby sisters' complicated puzzle—or if there really was someone dangerous lurking in the shadows.

"Katherine will be in the hospital for at least the night," he told me. "They are going to treat her for poisoning and hopefully she'll be alright. But tonight will be touch and go. Sorry this happened," he said and squeezed my hand. His big palm was so comforting in mine. I longed to reach out and pull him in, but he was on duty and I knew it wasn't the right time. So I took a deep breath and dropped his hand, knowing that we would be able to hold each other later.

"I'd better get over to the station. Did you come with someone? Do you need a ride?" He looked around, suddenly realizing the oddness of me being at the theater. "Why are you here, anyway?"

I laughed, despite the somber mood of the place. Here I was at yet another crime scene. Go figure. "I gave the sisters a ride over, so I can drive myself back. And I'm catering a party here at the end of the production, so I wanted to get that settled, which is why I'm here."

He nodded. "Alright, I'll try to call you tonight but it's touch and go with all this, so I'm not sure."

I glanced around and leaned into him for a quick kiss when I saw that nobody was watching us. "Okay. Good luck," I told him as he turned and walked down the hall toward the exit. Only after he left did I realize I'd forgotten to mention that video. It was probably way too late by now, though, so I let it go. With the way the internet was, either the news was all over the place or it had been drowned out by a million other happenings.

Looking around, I realized that the hall was nearly empty at this point. I'd wanted to speak with Charles about the party, but I had a feeling now wouldn't be a good time. But as I was about to leave, I spotted him at the end of the hallway near the theater entrance, talking to Ruth.

Curiosity got the better of me, and I slowed down as I moved through the hallway, pretending to adjust my purse strap as I eaves-dropped.

"Now we probably won't have a production at all," Charles was saying, his voice tight with frustration.

Ruth frowned. "But surely we have a backup plan? What about the understudy?"

Charles let out a bitter laugh. "You mean Brittney? She's barely able to remember her lines as it is, even though she's been prac-ticing for a month." He ran a hand through his hair, clearly agitated. "I mean, she's a sweet kid, and she looks the part, but I never really expected her to have to step in. This was supposed to be Katherine's triumphant return, you know?"

"But if Katherine can't perform..." Ruth began.

"Then I suppose Brittney will have to do," Charles cut her off, his tone making it clear he wasn't thrilled about the prospect. "God knows we can't afford to cancel the show. But it won't be the same. It won't have the star power we were banking on."

Conflicting emotions laced his voice. There was frustration, certainly, but also a hint of something else when he spoke about Brittney. Concern? Affection? I wasn't sure.

Ruth patted his arm sympathetically. "We'll make it work, Charles. We always do."

Charles nodded, but the tension in his shoulders didn't ease. I decided I'd heard enough and started to make my way towards the exit. I'd been at the Sugar Creek theater long enough already. I couldn't wait to get out into the sunshine, get some fresh air, get out of the uncomfortable vibes that seemed to waft from every corner of the place. How could people want to be here with all the drama and stress? I couldn't imagine, but clearly some didn't mind.

As I pushed open the heavy doors and stepped outside, I took a deep breath of fresh air, grateful to be leaving the tense atmosphere behind. I'd follow up about the catering job another time. For now, I had plenty to worry about.

Chapter Nine

Getting back into Aunt Meg's sedan, I puzzled over everything that had happened before shaking my head and starting the engine. Here we were with another mysterious death in Sugar Creek. And despite my desire to leave it alone and stay out of Ryan's way, my mind poured over everything that had happened, unable to let go of my curiosity. If the sisters were poisoned, then almost certainly someone had done it maliciously. But who?

I wouldn't be surprised if it turned out to be the house manager, Charles. His only concern seemed to be the theater, though, so it didn't immediately make sense. Why would he sabotage his own production by taking out the star? But there was an interesting dynamic between him and Katherine that I'd picked up on, too. Did it mean he wanted her gone? The cover of the production would make for a good shield to cover up a crime, should he have chosen to do away with her.

There was the understudy, Brittney, too. She seemed to be a nice girl, but Charles had said that she'd been practicing for a while for the role. And now that I thought about it, there was something off about the way Charles and Brittney interacted. Could there be more between them than a professional relationship? If so, that might give them both motive to want Katherine out of the picture, either to advance her career or to revenge some old hurt that Charles might have. Or both.

As I turned off Main Street to head back to Primrose House, I thought about the Drama Mamas again. They gave me pause as well, especially after the cold calculating conversation I'd overheard. But what motivation would any of them really have to kill Katherine? Nothing immediately apparent other than the possibility of increased publicity from the death. Although I thought having a Broadway star in their production already went a long way toward this goal, so why kill someone for more publicity?

Another possibility was that someone else from Sugar Creek had tried to kill her, someone from her past. But I had no idea what her life had been here, so I wouldn't even know where to start with this line of questioning.

And then there was Katherine's stalker—or at least, her belief that she had one. Could it be that she wasn't just being paranoid? Maybe someone really was following her, and this wasn't just some personal vendetta or theater rivalry. A stalker would have a completely different motive, but would that explain why Kelly had been poisoned, too? Katherine was the one who seemed convinced she was being followed, yet it was Kelly who died. Did the poison get to the wrong sister?

Unfortunately, I didn't know the theater crowd at all, so my theories were coming up pretty short other than the Drama Mamas, Charles, Brittney, and now the possibility of a stalker. I just hoped that Ryan would be able to make more progress than I had. And I hoped that he would be kind enough to share his theories with me once he had them, although he and Ty seemed to be playing things pretty close to the chest so far.

I pulled back into the parking lot of Primrose House and noticed that clouds had begun to gather. It was still way too warm for snow, but even a rain shower would go a long way toward putting me into a holiday mood. Those clouds made me immediately crave a peppermint mocha and a crackling fireplace.

I sighed as I parked Aunt Meg's sedan in a spot near the back of the lot. So much had happened. I would have to go in and tell Aunt Meg all about it, tell her that we were down one guest permanently and possibly two, if Katherine didn't pull through, or if she decided to go back home. Which wouldn't surprise me after what had happened.

Aunt Meg had been through so much over the past year with murders and guests that I worried how the news might affect her, how it might dampen the Christmas spirit of the B&B. I glanced at the pine garland that someone had wrapped around the porch rail and the beautiful handmade wreath hanging on the B&B door, and my heart sank. Christmas had always been so special to Aunt Meg, even after she started the B&B in our old farmhouse. Once my brother Devon and I were grown up and gone, she filled our void with guests and locals for parties and fun.

This year, though, things might be different. It all depended on what happened with Katherine Kirby. Would she return to the theater and to the B&B? Or would she flee this town and process her grief elsewhere? Only time would tell.

I hated to be the one to bear the bad news back here, but it wasn't to be helped. Aunt Meg would know eventually whether I told her or someone else did it.

So I climbed out of the car and headed inside to give her the news.

After a minute of poking around Primrose House, I finally found Aunt Meg and Maria in the backyard. The cool air nipped at my cheeks as I stepped outside, and a shiver ran up my spine.

Aunt Meg and Maria were wrestling with a massive metal contraption in the center of the lawn, both of them red-faced from exertion but grinning like kids on Christmas morning. Maria's dark hair had escaped a tidy bun, wisps framing her face as she laughed at something Aunt Meg said. Despite the chill in the air, they both had a warm glow about them, clearly enjoying the task at hand.

"Come on, Maria," Aunt Meg huffed, "let's get it, girl! Put your back into it!"

Maria, her eyes twinkling, gave an exaggerated groan. "Miss Meg, if I put any more of my back into it, I won't have any back left!"

It warmed my heart to see them like this, working together and having fun despite the usual stress of running the B&B, which made my news even more difficult to share. I sighed and pasted a smile on my face as I headed toward them.

"Look what we found!" Aunt Meg called out when she spotted me, her breath visible in the air. She and Maria gave the fire pit one final tug, positioning it perfectly on the grass. "Got it on a discount at the hardware store!"

Maria straightened up, brushing her hands on her jeans. "Abby, come help me convince your aunt that we don't need to roast an entire pig over this thing," she said with a wink.

"Don't give her any ideas," I laughed, but my smile faded as I remembered why I was here. The weight of the news I had to deliver suddenly felt very heavy indeed.

As I approached, the rich scent of earth filled my nostrils. The clouds were thicker now, and the air took on a heavy moisture that I felt in my bones. I buried my face in the neck of my sweater, and I found myself again longing for the warmth of a crackling fire. Maybe Aunt Meg's impulse purchase wasn't such a bad idea after all.

"It's nice," I said with a smile as I got closer. I glanced at the new Adirondack chairs littering the yard. Seemed like Aunt Meg had found an early Christmas present for herself. "What's it for?"

"I was thinking we could do a big fire on Friday evening, have some s'mores for guests, maybe open it up to the town if anyone wants to join. Get the festive spirit going. And Maria and I were thinking we could do a trial run tomorrow night as part of happy hour!" I could just picture a group of people around the yard, the smell of smoke and the delight of kids getting all hopped up on sugar. The fire pit was a perfect idea.

She adjusted the pit a little more and then straightened and brushed her hands together, then stopped as she saw the look on my face. "What's the matter? You don't like s'mores? We could do something else!"

"No. That's not it at all. I have some bad news." I slumped down into the chair and put my head in my hands, taking a deep breath before I said, "Katherine's in the hospital. I guess she was poisoned, but not enough to kill her. At least that's what we're hoping. But..." I said and then looked up to meet their eyes. "Kelly was poisoned too, and she didn't make it."

After I delivered the bad news about Katherine and Kelly, Aunt Meg's eyes turned down, and I noticed the unshed tears gathering in her eyes. My heart ached for her. Death was always hard, but for Aunt Meg, the death of a guest must really hit hard, especially since it wasn't the first time.

Oh, what a year it had been for us all.

I stood and moved over to Aunt Meg, giving her a long hug. She sighed against me, her shoulders feeling bony and frail in my embrace. Maria met my gaze over Aunt Meg's head, her eyes glittering with unshed tears as she wrapped her arms around herself. I hated being the bearer of bad news, but they had to know.

"Don't worry, girlie," she said after a minute and stepped out of my arms, quickly brushing a few tears away. "Things are going to be alright. We'll focus on the guests we do have tonight and try to make their holiday as magical as possible. And if Katherine returns, we'll try to help her out any way we can."

I nodded, but my mind was spinning. Glancing at my watch, I realized how behind I was. I still had cookie trays to prep and deliver, and my butter run had been totally forgotten after everything that happened at the theater, so I needed to make another trip out.

"I really need to get back to the kitchen," I admitted, feeling torn between helping Aunt Meg and tackling my growing to-do list. "I haven't even started the prep work for today's deliveries. I was supposed to stop by the store for butter, but..."

Aunt Meg waved her hand dismissively. "We'll be fine, Abby. You go take care of your business. We'll manage."

I wanted to believe her, but guilt gnawed at me. Aunt Meg was trying to hold everything together, keep the holiday spirit alive at the B&B, and here I was, running off to deal with catering. But if I didn't stay on top of my work, I'd be in financial trouble soon enough.

"Alright," I said reluctantly, "but if you need anything at all, call me. I'll be back in a flash if you do."

With one last glance at Aunt Meg and Maria, I headed for the door, mentally rearranging my to-do list. Butter, prep the rest of the cookies, deliveries, and then back to the B&B for more party prep work if I could swing it. No time for cozy fires or relaxing—just the reality of juggling everything at once.

CHAPTER TEN

My shoulders sagged as I made my way into the kitchen, the weight of the last few hours finally settling in like an overstuffed casserole dish I could barely carry. The shock of Kelly's death, the sadness hanging over the theater like a dark curtain—it was all catching up to me now. This morning, I'd imagined a holiday season full of joy, with festive gatherings, happy guests at Primrose House, and moments spent with friends over too many sugar cookies. But now, it felt like everything had shifted. Hardship and creeping sorrow seemed poised to seep into all our lives, casting a shadow over the holiday cheer.

I sighed, letting the familiar warmth of the kitchen pull me back into the present. The comforting smell of cinnamon and cloves lingered in the air, and I tried to focus on what I needed to do next. Party trays. Sandwiches. Focus on the task at hand, Abby.

But first, I needed to let Cassie know what had happened. She was going to find out one way or another, and she'd never forgive me if I didn't tell her right away. I pulled out my phone, fingers hesitating over the screen for a second, before I typed:

Me: Have some bad news... Someone died at the theater...

It only took a moment for the reply to come through.

Cassie: What?! You at the B&B? I'm coming over.

I exhaled slowly, my heartbeat calming slightly at the thought of seeing her soon. She always had a way of making things feel a little less... heavy.

Me: Yeah. Can you bring whatever butter is in the fridge when you come? Desperate over here...

I hit send, pocketing my phone, and looked around the kitchen again. Butter might not fix everything, but it would at least help with the trays I still had to make. Work had always been my way of coping, even when I didn't know what I was coping with.

I grabbed the bread from the pantry and set it on the counter, then pulled out trays for assembling sandwiches. My hands moved automatically, grabbing the ingredients I'd prepped the night before: thinly sliced turkey and ham, sharp cheddar, and crisp lettuce from the garden. The motions of buttering bread, layering ingredients, and wrapping each sandwich neatly in parchment paper were soothing, giving my mind a break from the heavier thoughts of the day.

Still, every so often, my mind drifted back to Kelly and what had happened at the theater, but I willed myself to focus on the food instead.

The kitchen door creaked open, and I glanced up, half expecting Cassie, but it was just Maria, bustling through with a tray of dirty dishes from earlier. "Need any help?" she asked, glancing at the half-assembled sandwiches.

"No, I've got it." I gave her a small smile, grateful but also wanting to be alone with my thoughts for a little longer. "Thanks, though."

She nodded and slipped back out, leaving me to the hum of the fridge and the steady rhythm of my own work. I pressed the next sandwich together, wrapping it neatly and placing it on the tray, lining each one up with military precision. As the tray filled, I felt a small, familiar sense of satisfaction—at least this was something I could control.

The back door banged open suddenly, and I nearly dropped the tray. Cassie stormed in, her eyes wide, holding a box of butter in one hand and her phone in the other. "Abby," she said, her voice a mix of disbelief and concern, "whoa, sister! You look like you got sandpapered! What the heck is going on?"

I wiped my hands on my apron, taking the butter from her and placing it on the counter. "Someone died over at the theater a while ago. Katherine Kirby's sister. Looks like it might have been murder."

Her hand flew to her mouth, and she sank onto a barstool, her eyes wide. "Oh, no. This is terrible! Don't tell me you found her!"

I shook my head, grateful that at least this time I wasn't the one to discover the body. "No, it was one of the theater people, but I was right there and I called it in. It wasn't just Kelly, either. Katherine was sick too. It looks like someone poisoned them. That's what Ryan thinks at least. Right now Katherine's at the hospital getting her stomach pumped and who knows what else."

"Poisoned? Who would poison them?"

Shrugging, I finished up the tray of sandwiches and closed the lid, then leaned back on the counter. "I don't know what happened yet. It happened in Katherine's dressing room, so it was probably meant for her, but Kelly is the one who died."

"Oh, man. I'm so sorry. That must have been rough."

"It's sad. I feel bad for her. Aunt Meg is taking it pretty hard, especially right now with Christmas so close. We aren't sure what's going to happen with Katherine yet."

Cassie's expression softened, and she pulled me into a quick hug. "I can't believe it. You okay?"

"Not really," I admitted, turning back to the sandwich trays. "But I'll get there. I just need to get these trays done for the clients."

"I have something that might help," Cassie said, her mouth quirking up in a smile. "Brought somebody to see you."

As soon as she said it, I heard a whimper at the door and I grinned, knowing that our little dog Cocoa was outside.

Cocoa was on me as soon as I walked out the door and I couldn't have been more happy to see his wiggling happy self. He was a bundle of delightful terrier energy and despite his small size, he could really throw his weight around so when he barreled into me, I was so overcome with emotion that I simply flopped down on the ground and took him in my arms, letting him lick my face before I rested my head on his side and sighed.

Cassie followed me outside, and we settled on the porch steps, Cocoa snuggled between us, his small body a bundle of warmth and comfort. The yard was still, the air cool and calm, in contrast to the storm of emotions swirling inside me. I ran my fingers through Cocoa's fur, but my mind couldn't settle.

"I can't believe this is happening again," Cassie said softly, breaking the silence. She glanced over at me, her brows knitted in concern. "Do they have any idea who might've done it?"

I shook my head, exhaling slowly. "They're looking into it, but there's this whole thing with Katherine... She's been talking about a stalker."

Cassie's eyes widened. "A stalker? In Sugar Creek?"

"Yeah, I know. It sounds dramatic, and honestly, I wasn't sure if I even believed her at first. She's been going on about someone following her. It was hard to tell if it was just her being paranoid, but now with Kelly dead, it's harder to brush off."

Cassie's expression turned serious as she processed this new information. "Okay, so if Katherine had a stalker, wouldn't they go after her? Why Kelly?"

"I don't know if she was necessarily the intended victim. The poison was in a bottle of champagne in Katherine's dressing room, so it was very likely meant for Katherine, not Kelly. An unhappy accident."

"Wow, that's rough."

I shrugged, my gaze drifting out to the yard. "I don't know.

But it's not just the stalker thing that's bothering me. There's this guy at the theater, Charles. He's the manager. There's something off about him, too."

"Really?" Cassie asked, leaning in, her interest piqued. "How so?"

"Well, when Katherine arrived, at first he was super friendly, calling her Kitty and trying to be close. But Katherine shut him down pretty fast and he turned really cold after that. I also saw him yelling at people and overheard some complaints. Nothing specific, but it all adds up to one very unhappy person."

Cassie let out a low whistle. "Sounds like a real piece of work."

"Yeah, it was weird. Like he had some kind of unresolved feelings about her—maybe jealousy or resentment. He just gave me bad vibes, you know? And now, with everything that's happened, I can't help but wonder if he's involved somehow."

Cassie tilted her head, thinking it over. "So, we've got a potential stalker, this Charles guy who seems to have some kind of grudge, and then there's the fact that Kelly's the one who ended up dead, not Katherine. What a mess."

"I know, right?" I agreed, running a hand through my hair. "And to top it off, there's this whole group at the theater—they call themselves the Drama Mamas. They basically run the local productions and are super invested in the theater. I don't know, maybe there's nothing to it, but I got a weird vibe from them, too. I overheard them talking after what happened and they seemed to almost be happy about it, thinking it would get the theater more publicity."

"That's cold," Cassie said, crossing her arms over her chest. "I mean, sure, everyone loves a little drama in theater, but using a death to boost ticket sales? No, thank you."

"Exactly," I said, resting my head against Cocoa's warm back. He panted and licked my hand. "It feels like everyone has their own angle, their own agenda. The stalker thing could be real, or maybe Katherine's just feeding into it for attention. Charles has

this weird, jealous energy, and the Drama Mamas are milking this
for all it's worth. I don't know who's responsible, but I don't trust
any of them."

Cassie was silent for a moment, her brow furrowed as she
processed everything. Finally, she spoke, her voice calm but determined. "It sounds like you've got a lot of pieces, but none of them
fit together yet. You think it's one of these people?"

I shrugged. "I don't know. It could be the stalker, it could be
Charles, it could be someone I haven't even thought of yet. I just
can't shake the feeling that there's more going on than what we see
on the surface."

Cassie nodded, her hand resting on Cocoa, who was now half-
asleep between us. "So, what's our plan of action?"

I frowned at her. But as much as I would love to pretend that
we were going to keep our distance from this thing, I knew as well
as she did that we would be in it as thick as the dew on Dixie in no
time.

"We could talk to one of the actors," I said, my mind suddenly
starting to whir to life with theories. "I met the one who's playing
the understudy role...is that what you call it? She was standing in
for Katherine."

Cassie nodded, her eyes already sparking with excitement.

"She seemed nice enough. But now that I'm thinking about it,
she seemed to have something going on with Charles too. I don't
know what their relationship is, or whether she would be open
with us, but it would be a place to start."

"Should we go now?"

"Oh, no. No way. I have way too much to do. It'll have to
wait."

Cassie sighed and bounced her leg on the step. "When'll you
be done, you think?"

I looked at my watch, and my heart did a little flip. "Never, if
we keep yapping."

She smacked my leg, and I grinned. "I have a few drop offs to do today, but I should be done around dinnertime."

"You have any idea how we might get in touch with this actress? See if she'd be willing to talk?"

I frowned and looked out on the cold grey afternoon. "I have no idea. I guess we could stop by the theater again, although I don't really want to do that. Let me finish up and think about it. I'll text you *if* I have any spare time after I get my work done."

"Okay, I've got to get back to the shop, too. But call me if you hear anything at all, alright? Mandy's at the shop all week, so it's no problem for me to pop in and out if need be."

I nodded and sighed as I looked out to the yard where the fire-pit was all set up and ready for Aunt Meg's big plans. "Boy, I have a mountain of work to get done," I muttered under my breath.

Cassie leaned over and gave me a quick hug. "Hang in there, lady. When we get home tonight, maybe we can throw on our comfiest pjs, crack a bottle of wine, and watch a Christmas movie."

I grinned and hugged her back. "That sounds fantastic. I'm counting on it."

Cassie nodded and stood and Cocoa did the same, stretching and wagging his tail before following her out to the lot. I felt a little bit better as I watched them go. Maybe we weren't any closer to solving the mystery yet, but with Cassie by my side, I knew I wasn't facing it alone.

Chapter Eleven

I couldn't think of a worse time for Kelly's murder to have happened. It was an insensitive thought because, of course, there was no *good* time for anyone to be murdered. But I had so much to do—parties in every direction, cookie trays needing to be baked, boxed up, and delivered, not to mention all the Christmas stuff with friends and family. I didn't have a minute to spare for sleuthing with Cassie, no matter how much I wanted to.

Of course, despite me trying my best to shut Cassie's sleuthing tendencies down, the universe had other ideas.

On my final stop to drop off cookie trays, Lisa, the costume designer from the theater, answered the door. Her face lit up when she saw me.

"Hey, I didn't realize this was your place!" I said, offering her a warm smile as I held up the tray.

"It's not. It's my sister's house," she replied, stepping aside as another woman—tall and slim, with the same long hair as Lisa—appeared in the doorway.

"Oh, good! The cookies!" the woman said with a relieved sigh.

Just then, a pack of wild children barreled down the stairs like a tiny stampede. The word "cookies" had summoned them, and they crowded around, howling for sweets. I handed over the tray just in time to avoid being mobbed, laughing as the kids swarmed the other woman.

"Come on in," Lisa's sister said, moving toward the back of the house, the children orbiting around her like hyperactive satellites.

I stepped inside, and Lisa closed the door behind me.

"How are you holding up?" I asked, suddenly remembering the murder at the theater earlier that day. Kelly Kirby, dead right at the theater. It must have been rattling for everyone involved with the production.

Lisa sighed and glanced toward the corner where a sewing machine sat, surrounded by scraps of fabric. "I'm okay, I guess. It's been... weird." She hesitated, then gestured toward the half-finished costumes draped over the chair. "I feel bad for the Kirby sisters. I mean, what a horrible thing to happen right before opening night."

I nodded, my heart sinking for Kelly's sister, Katherine. They'd barely been back in town a week, and now one of them was dead.

Lisa rubbed her hands together and continued. "Charles is still determined to carry on with the show, even if Katherine can't perform. He's been pushing us to keep going as planned. He's even got me working overtime to finish all the costumes."

I raised my eyebrows. "Even after everything?"

"Yep." Lisa gave a wry smile. "He doesn't seem too shaken up by it all. Actually, he's more focused than ever. I guess he thinks the show *has* to go on. Although that could be pressure from the Drama Mamas. I know they have very strong opinions about not cancelling, even if it means Brittney at the helm."

"What do you think?"

She shrugged. "I'd love to get paid for the work I've already done. I feel really bad for the Kirby sisters, I do. And I know it'll be a little weird to be back at the theater after what's happened. But I think there isn't much sense in cancelling the whole thing, just because Katherine's sister died."

I understood her point of view. The group had worked very hard to make the Christmas performance work and now, so close to opening night, the threat of having to shut it all down must be awful for them all.

"Well, I hope it all gets sorted and things work out for y'all." I stood up, and she walked me to the door. "Hey, would you mind sharing my contact info with Brittney when you get a chance? I'd love to drop in on her, maybe take her a few cookies, see how she's doing after everything."

It hadn't been my plan before, but suddenly Cassie's sleuthing urges came to mind and I got an idea.

"Oh, sure! I'm sure she'd love that. She doesn't have much. I worry about her sometimes. But she's young. She'll find her way." She sent Brittney a text and a moment later, I got a reply from Brittney that, of course, she would love some cookies. Luckily, I'd brought a small box of extras I'd planned to share with Cassie. I was sure she wouldn't mind sharing them for the sake of a little investigating.

I said goodbye to Lisa and walked back out into the chilly night. It hadn't rained yet, but the clouds still hung warm and damp over everything.

My mind turned to motive as I headed back to the van. Who would have gained from Kelly—or, more likely, Katherine—dying? The event was a toss-up as far as the outcome for the theater. It could lead to the show being cancelled or to it gaining in popularity. I doubted anybody would murder for such a murky possible outcome, but who knew? Brittney might benefit if she got to be the star of the show. That seemed like a real motive. Charles was a big cloud of confusion for me too, though. On the one hand, he seemed to have a grudge against at least Katherine and maybe both of the sisters. But taking one or both of them out jeopardized the show that he'd worked so hard to pull off. Would he dare? Why not wait until after the show was over?

If it was a stalker, of course, all bets were off. Who knew what motivated a stalker, but I doubt it had anything to do with theater business one way or the other.

The bell over the door of Divine Finds jingled as I stepped inside a few minutes later, the scent of sandalwood and cinnamon greeting me as I scanned the shelves full of vintage treasures and quirky antiques. Cassie was behind the counter, chatting with a customer, but she waved me over the moment she saw me.

After she finished ringing the woman up, I grinned at her, and she practically took flight. "Do you have something? Tell me you have something!"

I laughed. "Not much, but the understudy Brittney said she'd talk to us."

"How'd you pull that off?" Cassie asked.

"I bribed her with cookies."

Her eyes lit up with excitement. "Cool! Let's go!"

She gave instructions to her shop helper, Mandy, and then we headed out to my van.

Cassie buckled her seatbelt and turned to me, her mind already hard at work. "So what's the plan? What exactly are we going to ask Brittney?"

I gripped the wheel as I pulled away from the curb, thoughts swirling in my head. "I think we start by asking her if she saw anything, or if she knows anyone who would want to hurt the sisters. But I'm curious to get her take on both the Drama Mamas and Charles. I want to see if she knew anything about Charles and the sisters in the past, if they had any difficult history."

Cassie leaned back, nodding slowly. "That sounds good. We can watch her reactions, too. See if there's anything that gives her own intentions away."

"That's what I was thinking too," I agreed, speeding up slightly as the streets of Sugar Creek blurred past.

"I hope we get something."

I nodded. "Whatever she has to say, I bet there's something to learn," I replied, more to calm myself than Cassie. We both knew that when it came to small-town drama, there were always skeletons rattling somewhere in the closet. And I had a feeling we were about to open a big one.

We pulled up to Brittney's apartment complex, a beige, nondescript building with slightly weather-worn siding. It was one of those forgettable places you wouldn't notice unless you were looking for it. I double-checked the address and parked.

Cassie got out, and I grabbed the box of cookies and scanned the area, trying to shake off my growing sense of worry about the potential stalker. There was no reason to think the stalker might be after me, but I was on edge, nevertheless.

As we started toward the building, Cassie broke the silence. "Oh, I forgot to tell you, but I was talking to my cousin Melissa a little while ago—you remember Melissa?"

"Sure," I said, pushing open the main door to the complex.

"She went to school with the Kirby sisters, and when she heard what happened with Kelly, she gave me a call."

"Oh?" I raised my eyebrows. Cassie's cousin always had an ear to the ground when it came to small-town gossip.

"Apparently, things weren't easy for them growing up. Their dad left when they were young, and their mom... had a bit of a drinking problem."

I paused for a moment, processing that. "That tracks how they were talking in the car. They seemed to not have a very good childhood."

Cassie shook her head. "It's a shame. Melissa said Katherine and Kelly were always determined to get out of here and make something of themselves. And I guess they did."

We arrived at Brittney's door. Before I could knock, it swung open, revealing Brittney, phone in hand, her face barely made up but still as striking as ever.

"Oh! Hi! I thought you were someone else..."

"Hey, Brittney," I said, offering a small smile. "I have the cookies."

She beamed at me and took the box, then ushered us in.

Brittney's apartment was a mismatched hodgepodge of hand-me-down furniture and thrift store finds. The worn-out couch sagged in the middle, and a coffee table with chipped edges sat crooked in front of it. The walls were mostly bare except for a few crooked, unframed prints she'd thumbtacked up for color. The space felt more temporary than permanent, with boxes still tucked into corners, like she hadn't quite settled in—or didn't plan to.

"I wanted to stop by and talk to you about what happened with Kelly and Katherine. I know it's a lot to process, but I was hoping to get your take on it," I told her. She sat on the couch and frowned.

Brittney's eyes flickered with something—nerves, maybe?—and she shifted on the couch. "It's awful," she said, her voice wavering just slightly. "I mean, Kelly... I didn't know her super well, but she didn't deserve that. And Katherine... she's the big star, right? I can't believe something like this happened to them both."

"I know. It was quite a shock. I wondered if you saw or heard anything that might be useful."

I debated telling her about our relationship with the police department, but decided against it. I wanted her to think of us as friends, not people digging for information.

She shrugged and fiddled with the string on the box of cookies. "I didn't see much. Charles said they were poisoned with champagne that was left in the dressing room. It must've been awful."

I glanced at Cassie. "Are you and Charles close?"

Brittney hesitated for just a beat, her hand still playing with the string. "Oh, not really," she said, her voice casual, but her body language betrayed something more. She tucked her hair behind her ear, avoiding eye contact. "We only met when he hired me for the Christmas play. He's nice enough, I guess."

But the way she shifted on the couch, her eyes darting toward the kitchen and back to us, told me there was more to the story.

Her casual dismissal didn't match the tension in her shoulders. I exchanged a quick look with Cassie. Something was going on between them—whether Brittney wanted to admit it or not.

"Did you know that Charles and the Kirby sisters knew each other in high school?" I asked.

Brittney's eyebrows rose slightly, but she tried to mask her reaction. "I mean, I heard some rumors, but I don't know any details. They don't seem to like each other much, though."

"What gives you that impression?"

"Just the way they acted toward each other. Like there was some bad history there." Brittney shrugged again, but her eyes flickered with interest, as if she knew more than she was letting on.

"And what about the Drama Mamas?" Cassie asked, her voice light but probing.

Brittney smiled, her guard lowering just a little. "Oh, they're harmless. And so sweet! Always complimenting me. I think they're rooting for me to get the part if Katherine doesn't pull through." She paused, looking almost hopeful for a second, before she caught herself.

I glanced at Cassie before continuing, trying to get a feel for how Brittney was really feeling. "It must've been hard, watching her come in and take over the lead. Especially after you've worked so hard."

Brittney hesitated for a moment, then shrugged. "It was hard, yeah. I've been the understudy for a month now. I've been working my butt off. Then Katherine swoops in, and suddenly, it's like no one else matters. But..." she glanced down, biting her lip before continuing, "that's the job, right? If she doesn't recover, I guess it'll be my chance to step up."

There it was—a flash of excitement in her eyes that she quickly tried to hide. She shrugged. "It's not that big of a deal either way. There's always another show to do. Christmas is a big one, but it wouldn't be the end of the world if it was canceled."

Her tone didn't match her words. She wanted the play to go

through, and she wanted the main role. Her voice made it clear, even if her words didn't. But was it enough for her to have killed someone for?

I glanced at Cassie, and she nodded. "Well, thanks for talking to us," I said, standing up. "I know it's a tough time, but I appreciate you giving us your perspective."

Brittney nodded too, still looking a little unsure. She opened the lid to the cookies and eyed them before closing the box back up. "Yeah, no problem. I just hope everything works out. With Katherine and all that. And the play."

Brittney gave us a polite smile as we stood to leave, though she seemed relieved we were going. "Thanks for stopping by," she said, opening the door for us.

"Thanks for the chat," I replied, giving her a small nod as I stepped out into the hallway. Cassie followed behind me, her hands stuffed in her pockets. "Take care," she muttered over her shoulder.

Brittney closed the door quietly behind us, and Cassie let out a small sigh as we made our way down the stairs. "Well, that was... interesting," she said under her breath, but I could tell she wasn't ready to get into it just yet.

We didn't say much as we headed outside. The air hit us with a damp chill, and I pulled my sweater tighter around myself as we stepped into the fading light.

CHAPTER TWELVE

A light patter of rain began as we left Brittney's apartment, and I pulled my thin sweater tighter around myself, shivering as we hurried to my van. The sky had taken on that flat gray tone that meant it would rain all night, and I felt a little of the weight of the day settling in.

Once we were inside the van, I rubbed my hands together, waiting for the heater to kick on. The cold air in the van felt sharper than it should have, and the rain pinged softly against the windshield. I sighed and leaned back in my seat. "What did you think?" I asked Cassie.

She didn't answer right away. Instead, she bit her lip and stared out the window, her eyes following the drops of rain as they streaked across the glass. "Interesting," she finally said, but her tone was thoughtful, not convinced. "I guess I'm not that surprised that Charles wants to keep the play going. I mean, that's why they have an understudy for Katherine, right?"

I nodded slowly, keeping my eyes on the road. "Yeah, I get that. But it still feels off."

Cassie turned to face me, her brow furrowing in concentration. "Exactly. Like something's going on underneath. I can't figure out what, though. There's something about him that just doesn't sit right. It's like... I don't know." She shrugged. "I wish I'd met him."

I shot her a sideways glance. "Trust me, you're not missing much."

Her eyes suddenly lit up, the way they always did when she had an idea she knew I wouldn't like. "Hey, what if we head over to the theater? I bet he's there, and we could..."

I was already shaking my head before she even finished. "Nope. Not tonight. We've done enough sleuthing for one day." I kept my tone firm, though the idea of seeing Charles again, even if just to observe him, did tempt me a little. Still, I wasn't about to admit that. "I agree. He's sketchy, but going over there to try to talk to him isn't going to get us anywhere. Trust me, the guy's a jerk. He won't tell us anything unless we flash cash in his face."

Cassie rummaged around in her purse dramatically, pulling out a couple of crumpled bills. "I've got fifty bucks! Maybe that'll loosen his tongue."

I shot her a glare so sharp she immediately raised her hands in surrender. "Okay! Okay! No bribing the potential suspect."

I laughed despite myself, shaking my head as I pulled out of the parking lot. Rain dripped steadily off the trees lining the road, the streetlights casting a hazy glow in the mist. Cassie folded her arms, leaning her forehead against the cool window, her voice a little more serious now. "But you saw how Brittney reacted when she mentioned his name, right? I bet they're sleeping together."

I nodded, navigating the quiet streets toward Main. "I thought so too. She seemed a little too defensive."

Cassie sighed. "Yikes. That's gotta complicate things. Think she knows something she's not telling us?"

"Maybe." I turned onto Main Street, passing the familiar line of shops and restaurants that made up the heart of Sugar Creek. The rain was coming down a little heavier now, casting the whole town in a cozy blur. We were passing Ling's Chinese Restaurant when Cassie perked up again.

"Ooh! Let's stop at Ling's! I'm starving. Some takeout and a good movie sound perfect right now."

I didn't need much convincing. My stomach growled in agreement as I pulled into the parking lot. "Egg rolls and General Tso's, here we come."

Fifteen minutes later, we were driving back to Cassie's place, bags of takeout warming our laps and Cocoa waiting eagerly for us at home. As soon as I unlocked the door, Cocoa bounded over, hopping and barking as if we'd abandoned him for a week instead of just a few hours.

"Oh, poor baby!" Cassie cooed, scooping him up as he wiggled in excitement. "I can't believe we left him in the dark!"

I flicked on the lights, setting our food on the kitchen counter. "He was probably napping the whole time," I teased, watching as Cocoa darted back and forth between us, his tail wagging so hard his whole body shook.

Cassie laughed and reached for the wine glasses. "Okay, food and wine. Then we can get back to solving the mysteries of Sugar Creek."

We settled in on the couch, legs tucked under blankets, the rain tapping gently on the windows as we unpacked our takeout. Cocoa curled up at our feet, finally content now that his humans were back.

"So," Cassie said between bites of fried rice, "what do you think? *It's a Wonderful Life* or *Elf*?"

I took a sip of wine, considering it. "What about *Miracle on 34th Street*? It feels like that kind of night."

Cassie grinned. "Yes! Perfect choice." She flipped on the TV and pulled up the movie while I burrowed deeper into the cushions. With a full glass of wine in hand, food on my lap, and Cocoa snoring softly at our feet, I couldn't imagine a more perfect way to spend the evening.

———

The doorbell rang a little after eleven and by the way Cocoa yipped excitedly I had a feeling I knew who was at the door. Cassie and I jumped up after pausing Elf and pulled ourselves together the best we could. We were both in our pjs by this point and well into our bottle of wine. I brushed a piece of popcorn out of my hair as she looked through the peephole and grinned.

Opening the door, Ryan and Ty came in, both of them still in uniform. Ryan grabbed me and pulled me into a long hug and a kiss and finally, finally, I felt whole.

"What a day," he whispered into my neck. Cocoa bounced around beneath us all, running back and forth to lick both Ryan and Ty. All his people were present, and he was a happy pup. I knew the feeling.

I nodded and glanced over at Cassie and Ty, who were stuck in a similar embrace. "You guys want a beer? Or are you still on the clock?" I asked as I grabbed Ryan's hand and guided him over to one of the barstools.

He nodded gratefully and sank down into the seat. I grabbed one for each of them and then poured Cassie and me another glass of wine.

I sat next to Ryan and Cassie and Ty sank down onto the couch and turned toward us. "What happened? Do you know yet if it was poison? Is Katherine okay?" I asked.

Ryan took a long drink and nodded. "They were both poisoned. Kelly died, as you know. Katherine was treated, and it looks like she'll be okay. I was able to talk with her quite a bit this evening and got her side of the story."

He took another drink, and we waited as he gathered his thoughts a moment before continuing. "She said that a bottle of champagne was there in her dressing room when they went back for Katherine to get ready for rehearsal and that she was sure it had still had the cork in it. She saw Kelly remove the cork herself, so

I'm inclined to think that whatever poisoned them wasn't in the champagne at all, but maybe in something else. It might have been in the glasses or on the strawberries that were in the room, too. We'll have to wait to hear back from the lab for sure. They are testing everything that was in that room, so it'll take a while. But whatever it was, the sisters were definitely poisoned."

Cassie's face turned down, and she pulled Ty closer. I took a sip of the wine and thought back to that scene in the dressing room, trying to remember anything that might be useful but coming up blank.

"Do you have any ideas about who or why yet?" I asked him gently.

"Katherine says that she's picked up a stalker recently, and I checked with the police in New York and confirmed that she's made several complaints about a man harassing her at home and work. Her theory is that someone was really after *her*, not her sister. That maybe this person followed them from New York, which very well may be true. It was clearly Katherine's dressing room and whoever left that bottle wouldn't have immediately assumed that Kelly would have been there too, I imagine. But other than having a strong suspicion that Katherine was the target, I don't really know. We have so many leads to follow up on, my head is spinning."

He sighed, and I rubbed his hands in my own, wishing I could make things easier for him. But of course, I couldn't.

I nodded as I processed everything he said. "Yeah, I was thinking Katherine was the likely target, too. And she was talking a blue streak about her stalker from the minute she arrived at the B&B yesterday. I didn't know if I believed her at first, but now..."

"It's not the only lead, but it's a strong one."

"Did y'all see anything unusual when you processed the room?" Cassie asked.

Ty and Ryan exchanged a glance, and I knew they were silently debating whether to tell us anything about the investigation. Given our history of snooping and causing trouble when it came to murder, I didn't fault them for their hesitation.

"Nothing much, other than the champagne and strawberries. We talked to the house manager, Mr. Charles Dunhill, but he wasn't sure who had given the food and champagne to the women. Unfortunately, the theater isn't particularly secure and there aren't any cameras inside the building, so it's going to be very hard to tell who went in and out of that room other than the sisters."

"Ugh, that makes things really difficult. So I guess motive is a good place to start weeding people out?" I asked.

Ryan sighed and nodded, running a hand through his hair. "We're planning to do a few more in-depth interviews over at the theater tomorrow, see if we can drill down on anything."

"It's going to be a long day tomorrow," Ty added, finishing his beer. "But hopefully, we'll start to piece together a clearer picture of what happened and why."

I nodded, feeling a mix of concern and curiosity. Part of me wanted to help, to dig into the mystery myself, but I knew Ryan and Ty would prefer if I stayed out of it. Still, I couldn't help but wonder what secrets might be lurking in the sisters' past here in Sugar Creek.

As if reading my mind, Ryan finished his beer and set the bottle down with a sigh. His expression turned serious as he looked at Cassie and me. "Listen, I need to say something important. You two need to stay out of this. I'm not kidding around here."

Ty nodded in agreement, his arm tightening around Cassie's shoulders.

Ryan continued, his voice firm. "With all the reporters poking around and the threat of the feds stepping in if we can't get our act together, I need this investigation to be clean as a whistle. There is not going to be any meddling this time, do y'all understand?"

I felt a flicker of disappointment. All of a sudden, I felt like we were going back in time. "But what about all the times we've helped? You said we were helpful yourselves!" I said, remembering how our collaboration had helped solve so many other mysteries.

"Things are too serious this time, y'all," Ty chimed in, backing up Ryan. "We can't have any interference."

Cassie and I exchanged glances, a mix of frustration and understanding passing between us. I could see the wheels turning in Cassie's head, probably already plotting ways around this directive.

"We understand," I said slowly, trying to keep the disappointment out of my voice. "It's just... we care about this town too, you know? And Katherine. It's hard to just sit back and do nothing."

Cassie nodded and arched her eyebrows. "Exactly! Plus, we have connections in town that you might not. We could be helpful."

Ryan's expression softened slightly, but he shook his head. "I know you both want to help, and I appreciate that. But this time, the best way you can help is by staying out of it. Please."

I sighed, knowing he was right, but not liking it one bit. "Okay, we'll try our best to stay out of it. But if we happen to hear something..."

"Then you'll tell us immediately and let us handle it," Ty replied.

Ryan glanced at Ty and nodded. "Alright, we should head out. Early day tomorrow," he said as he stood.

Cassie crossed her arms, watching them both with a mix of frustration and fondness. "Yeah, well, don't work too hard," she said, though her eyes showed she was still bristling at the directive to stay out of the investigation.

"We'll try," Ty said, flashing a grin as he pulled on his coat.

Ryan reached for me and, despite my frustration about his warning, I leaned in for a kiss. Cocoa, not wanting to be left out of goodbyes, circled our feet, tail wagging. Ryan chuckled and bent down to give him a good scratch behind the ears. "Take care of these ladies for us, buddy," he said, eliciting an excited yip from Cocoa.

Ryan opened the door, and the cold night air rushed in, carrying with it the soft patter of the ongoing rain. He turned back to us, his expression softening a little. "Seriously, you two—stay safe. We'll figure this out. And if you hear anything, call us."

"Got it," I replied, knowing full well Cassie wasn't going to let it go so easily.

Ty patted Cocoa's head one last time before stepping outside. "Goodnight, ladies," he said, then gave a quick nod. "And thanks for the beer."

"Goodnight," Cassie and I said in unison, standing by the door as they walked out into the misty night.

Cassie shut the door on the cold and turned to me with a devious look. "You know we have to get involved now, don't you?"

I grinned and nodded. Staying out of the investigation was the last thing I planned to do now.

CHAPTER THIRTEEN

The next morning I woke early, ready for the mountain of prep work and cookie trays that called my name. Cocoa stretched lazily and rolled over on his back as I climbed out of bed. Clearly, he had no interest in my early morning plans. I laughed as I patted his belly and then took a quick shower and got dressed for the day ahead in jeans, a t-shirt, and sneakers, my regular prep day attire.

Moving into the kitchen, I poured myself a cup of coffee, adding a generous splash of white chocolate mocha creamer, grateful that Cassie had already started the pot. The rich aroma helped clear some of the fog from my brain.

As much as I hated the idea that I was intruding by living with Cassie, she had absolutely insisted that she wanted me to stay with her until the wedding so after a small stint where I'd watched over the B&B for Aunt Meg while she was away visiting her cousin at the end of the summer, I'd moved back into Cassie's little bungalow. I was grateful for her generosity because my dwindling reserves of cash hadn't put me in a great position to shell out rent at the moment. But I was hoping that the holiday season would provide me with a money buffer because in March I would need to be in my own place so the newlyweds could move in together without me getting in their hair.

The main room of Cassie's place was taken up by an astounding mashup of Christmas and wedding paraphernalia. Ty had proposed to Cassie back in the summer and ever since then we'd been on a constant wedding merry-go-round of dresses, decorations, and of course, food. After plenty of plying by Aunt Meg and me, we'd finally convinced her to let us give her the gift of the venue and the food, but it was shocking to me how many more little details had to be ironed out in order to make the event, that was scheduled for the following spring, happen just right. I wasn't kidding when I'd told Ryan I didn't want a big wedding anymore. Cassie's wedding madness had shocked me right out of any interest.

"Morning, lady!" Cassie said when she came out of her room a few minutes later, already dressed in a vintage blouse and bell-bottoms with her blonde curls bouncing on her shoulders and jangling bangles making noise on her wrists. "You sleep okay?"

"I did! What about you?"

"Pretty well, although I had a lot on my mind."

I nodded, knowing the feeling.

"We aren't going to leave this thing to Ryan and Ty, right?" Cassie said as she poured herself another cup and added cream.

Frowning, I glanced out the window, where rain pattered softly on the window, and then I sighed. As much as I wanted to be good, to make Ryan happy, to follow the rules, I knew myself... and Cassie too well. "No."

"So, what's our plan going to be?"

"You said your cousin knew her in high school, right? Maybe we should pay her a visit, see if there's anything else she remembers that might be helpful. And if she knew Katherine, she probably knew Kelly and Charles, too."

"She's going to be at Ellie's baby shower. We could ask her then."

My eyes lit up. "That's great! I can work, while I work, while I party," I said with a laugh. "My best kind of work."

Cassie laughed too and then frowned. "Speaking of Charles, I wonder if we can find anything else out about him? He sounds pretty suspicious to me."

I leaned my elbows on the counter, deep in thought. "Huh. I guess if he's been here since high school, there should be plenty of people around who know him. I'll put some feelers out, see if I can find anyone."

Cassie grinned and nodded. "Good thinking! We need to tap into our resources, right? Show those guys we have something to add." Her voice was tinged with hurt, and I felt the same. After Cassie and I being so helpful for the last few murders, I would have thought they'd be happy to have our help. But instead, it felt like they were brushing us aside...now that the spotlight was on them. Did they want to protect their investigation? I was certain of it. But a small part of me wondered if they wanted all the glory for solving the case, too. It was a cynical thought, but I was in a cynical mood.

Nodding, I thought as I sipped my hot coffee, feeling the warmth of it travel down my spine. "It seems like there are a couple of different possibilities with this case," I mused. "One is that there's some stalker out to get Katherine. That seems like a police matter. It seems like something we could leave to the guys. But the other possibility is that it is something related to the town or the past. And that's what we're best at. So I say we focus on that side of things. So, in a way, we could say we're staying out of the investigation. At least as far as the stalker is concerned."

Cassie grinned deviously. "I like the way you think, sister."

I glanced at the clock and almost had a conniption. Too much to do, too little time.

"Alright, I'm heading out. Good luck with the shop today," I said, chugging the last bit of my coffee and grabbing my purse.

"Thanks, hon. Have a good one!"

I opened the door, only to find a massive camera in my face.

"Good morning Abby Hirsch. We're with KVUE News out of Austin. Care to comment on the attempted murder of Katherine Kirby?"

My first instinct was to slam the door in their faces, and that's exactly what I did.

"What's going on?" Cassie asked with a frown as I did it.

"Reporters," I told her with a grimace.

Her frown deepened. "Why are they *here*?"

I shrugged, but heard them through the door. "Miss Hirsch! We know you were the one to find the sisters! We'd love to have a word!"

Until that moment, I'd forgotten all about the video from the day before. But I guessed it had made the rounds and now I was known as the one to find the sisters. I wished I would have grabbed that phone and deleted the video when I'd had the chance. This was not the kind of publicity I needed or wanted.

"I forgot to tell you, but one of the young kids at the theater yesterday posted a video of what happened. I think I was in it."

Cassie made a face, and we both winced as a knock sounded on the door again, followed by a muffled, "Miss Hirsch, we just have a few questions! Can you tell us anything about Katherine Kirby's condition? Are the police still investigating?"

Cassie crossed her arms, a mischievous spark in her eyes. "Well, we could just push our way out. Show 'em what we're made of."

I almost laughed at that, but my stomach knotted at the thought of cameras in my face. I stared at the door, weighing my options. Slamming the door shut again wasn't going to work—they weren't going away. "Maybe I should just... make a dignified exit," I said, my voice laced with sarcasm. "No comment. Act like it's no big deal."

Cassie nodded, her grin fading into sympathy. "It's probably the smart move. If you ignore them long enough, they'll get bored and move on."

I sighed. She was right. "Great. I bet they're recording everything, and the last thing I want is to look like I'm hiding something."

I smoothed my hair down, forcing my shoulders to relax. "Okay. Here goes nothing. Dignity, poise, and absolutely no losing my cool."

"Good luck, lady," Cassie said with a grin. "You've got this! But text me when you get to the B&B so I know you got there safe!"

She leaned in and gave me a quick hug and Cocoa barked in agreement. I bent and pet him one last time, then steeling myself, I opened the door just wide enough to step out. Sure enough, the camera was back in my face. "Miss Hirsch! Could you share what you saw when you found Katherine Kirby and her sister?"

I raised my hand, feeling the weight of every camera trained on me. "I have no comment at this time," I said as firmly as I could, trying to keep my face neutral.

A flurry of follow-up questions hit me. "Are you involved in the investigation? Do you think she'll pull through? Any thoughts on the suspect?"

"I have no comment," I repeated, keeping my head high. I could feel my face flush under the pressure, but I turned away before they got to me.

They followed close behind as I got to my catering van and I ignored their questions and hounding the best I could as I unlocked the door and slid inside, finally sighing as I turned on the engine and felt the heater come on. I took a moment to collect myself and then slowly started to back out of my parking spot, careful not to hit anybody.

As I pulled out of Cassie's drive, the reporters finally shrinking in my rearview mirror, I thought about my long day of prep work ahead. Cookies and Christmas catering sounded a lot more pleasant than dealing with nosy reporters, and I planned to lose myself in it as soon as I could.

CHAPTER FOURTEEN

The clouds that had gathered the day before hung heavy over everything again this morning. I shivered as I grabbed my things and headed inside, saying a little prayer for a white Christmas as I went, although I didn't hold out much hope.

I was buzzing on coffee and ready to get to work. I had to wrap up work on a few trays for drop off clients and do more cookies. But my serious jobs didn't start until the following day and I was excited to work without feeling a ton of pressure.

When I walked in, I found Aunt Meg sitting near the fireplace with a couple of kids. They had a bowl of popcorn between them and she was demonstrating how to thread a needle through the kernels to make a popcorn wreath.

"Good morning!" I called out, shaking off the chill. "Looks like you've got some holiday elves on your hands."

Aunt Meg smiled warmly at me, squinting over her glasses as she focused on the popcorn string. "Morning, honey! I'm teaching these two how we used to do Christmas back in the day. They're naturals at this."

One of the kids—a girl with big, dark eyes—held up her work proudly. "I make long one!"

I smiled and gave her a thumbs up. "You sure did! Maybe I'll hire you to decorate one of my catering gigs."

Aunt Meg laughed and glanced up at me. "So, what's on your agenda today? Anything exciting, or just the usual chaos?"

"Oh, you know," I said, taking a deep breath and shifting my bags. "Some cookie trays to finish up, a few drop-offs, and if I have time, I'm going to give divinity a shot." I raised an eyebrow, feeling that old familiar twinge of doubt.

Aunt Meg chuckled, handing the little boy next to her another needle. "Good luck with that one. Divinity's trickier than a greased pig at a county fair."

I sighed dramatically. "Don't I know it. But it feels like a Christmas tradition, you know? I've got to at least try."

Aunt Meg grinned. "You'll get it. And if not, you'll at least have a good story to tell." She set the popcorn string down for a moment and gave me a more serious look. "By the way, have you heard anything about Katherine? Is she still in the hospital?"

My stomach tightened a little at the mention of Katherine. "No, nothing yet. I'm planning to stop by and see her in a while, though."

Aunt Meg gave me a quick pat on the shoulder as she headed toward the door. "Good luck with the divinity! Holler if you need anything."

The kitchen was cozy, already warm from the morning's activities. Maria stood at the sink, her hands deep in sudsy water as she worked through a pile of breakfast dishes. She looked up and smiled when she saw me.

"Hey, Abby. Looks like you're jumping into the storm today?"

I laughed, grabbing my apron from the hook. "You know it. But it's a light one today—no big deadlines until tomorrow, so I'm trying to enjoy the calm."

Maria nodded, drying her hands on a towel. "Better enjoy it

while it lasts. Did you see the sky? Feels like we're going to get snow or at least some kind of winter weather soon."

"I'm crossing my fingers for snow," I said, tying my apron. "But with my luck, we'll just get sleet. That'll make deliveries fun."

Maria chuckled. "Yep, nothing like sliding around on ice with a van full of sandwiches."

I smiled and pulled my notebook from my bag, flipping it open on the counter. Although my catering load seemed light today, I wanted to double-check my notes to make sure I hadn't forgotten anything before diving into the divinity project.

I scanned the list I'd made the night before, ticking off tasks with my finger: cookies, sandwiches, salads, and appetizers for a couple of corporate parties. Everything was prepped and ready to go except for a few assembly tasks that wouldn't take much time. Divinity was my wild card for the day, but as long as I managed that, I'd be in good shape.

Divinity is a finicky, old-timey dessert, but I'd always loved the fluffy white confection growing up. The thought of playing around with the traditional recipe tickled me, and I figured everyone else at Ellie's baby shower would feel the same. If it worked out, I might even add it to the theater party menu—assuming there was still a theater party, now that the star of the show was laid up in the hospital.

Thinking about the theater reminded me I still had to check in with Charles about the party and get a solid headcount. I didn't want to get too far into shopping or prep for that until I knew how many people I'd be feeding, and today was the day to start thinking about it seriously.

On top of that, I had cookie trays that needed to be baked and delivered this afternoon, plus some more planning for Ellie's party, which was only two days away. Maybe I didn't have time to fuss with divinity after all. But I couldn't help myself—it had a way of pulling me in.

First things first: I needed to finish the jobs I'd already scheduled. There was no way around it. I dove into the cookie trays, laying out the flour, sugar, butter, and spices. The kitchen quickly turned rich with the scent of vanilla and butter, and I couldn't help but smile, despite the work that lay ahead of me. If there was one thing that grounded me, it was baking.

I slid the first tray into the oven and set the timer, and then moved on to the sugar cookie dough. I planned to cut them into stars, bells, and trees, decorating them with icing and sprinkles to make them extra festive.

As I worked, my mind kept drifting back to the divinity. It was such a tricky dessert—finicky even under the best conditions. The egg whites had to be whipped to just the right stiffness, the sugar syrup cooked to exactly the right temperature. It was like trying to perform a magic trick, and I wasn't sure I had the time or patience for it today. But the challenge was part of the appeal. If I could pull it off, I knew it would be worth it.

The timer beeped, snapping me back to reality. I pulled the last tray of sugar cookies from the oven, pleased with how perfectly golden they were, and set them aside to cool. Next, I moved on to prepping the sandwiches for the corporate lunch—thin slices of turkey and ham, Swiss and cheddar, all layered onto fresh rolls I'd picked up earlier. I worked quickly, assembling and wrapping each sandwich in parchment paper, tying them off with twine for that extra holiday touch.

As I worked on the sandwiches, my mind wandered back to what had happened the day before. Kelly's sudden death from the poisoned champagne still had me rattled, and the fact that Katherine had barely survived wasn't something I could easily shake off. The whole thing was bizarre and terrifying—and I wondered if it had been a deliberate attack on both sisters or if Kelly had just been collateral damage.

As I placed the last sandwich in the box, I thought back to our conversation with Brittney the day before. She'd seemed shaken up when we talked, but there was something about her reaction that didn't quite sit right with me. She'd dropped hints about tension between Katherine and Charles, but I couldn't tell if she was being helpful or trying to steer me in a specific direction.

And then there was the way she talked about Charles—like there was something more between them than just work. I didn't have any solid evidence, but I had the distinct feeling there was some kind of relationship going on there. And if Brittney had a thing with Charles, what possibilities did that open up as far as motive was concerned? It was thorny and complicated and my mind couldn't make sense of it.

Thinking about Charles, I decided I might as well try calling him. I flipped through my notebook, looking for the contact information I'd jotted down for Charles at the theater. The party planning was still hanging in limbo, and now that Kelly was dead, who knew if the theater event would even happen? I needed a solid headcount, but I also wanted to talk to Charles about what had happened at the theater, if I could convince him to say anything. Maybe I could get a sense of what his real relationship with Katherine and Kelly was. He didn't seem to like her much, but I'd only overheard bits and pieces of conversations—nothing I could go on with confidence.

I pulled out my phone and dialed his number, the phone pressed to my ear as I loaded a container with salad and closed it up. It rang several times, then clicked over to voicemail.

"Hey, Charles, it's Abby from Deep in the Heart Catering. I just wanted to check in about the theater party and see if we're still moving forward. Give me a call when you can. Thanks."

I hung up, a little frustrated but not surprised, given how busy and uncooperative he'd been the day before. I couldn't shake the feeling that there was something more going on with Charles, Katherine, and Kelly. Had there been something deeper between them, something from the past? Or was that just the old high school rivalry Brittney had hinted at?

And then there was Brittney herself—now possibly stepping

into the role Katherine may or may not be physically able to take on now. That was a lot of good fortune for someone standing so close to the drama. Was it just coincidence?

I sighed, glancing at the clock. It felt like I was standing in the middle of a web, but I still didn't have enough threads to see the full picture. Katherine was the key, but she was stuck in the hospital, and now I had to wonder if she'd even be safe there. If someone had gone after her and Kelly once, what was stopping them from trying again?

I moved back to the counter, grabbing the last of the rolls and starting on the final tray. As much as I hated waiting for answers, I needed to keep my head down and finish what I could today. I'd try Charles again later, and maybe someone would slip up and give me a clue about what was really going on.

Finally, it was time for the divinity.

I set up my mixer and started with the egg whites, watching them whip into soft peaks. The sugar syrup was heating on the stove, bubbling away as I kept a careful eye on the thermometer. Divinity was all about timing and precision—too hot or too cold, and the whole batch would be ruined.

Just as the syrup reached the perfect temperature, I poured it in a thin stream into the egg whites, the mixer whirring at high speed. My heart raced a little as I watched, waiting for the moment when it would all come together. Slowly, the mixture thickened and turned glossy, transforming into something almost magical. I added a splash of vanilla and chopped pecans and kept the mixer running until the divinity reached the perfect consistency.

I scooped out small mounds of the candy onto a parchment-lined tray, feeling a wave of satisfaction. The batch had come out just right—fluffy, glossy, and sweet as a cloud. I smiled despite the lingering stress of the day. There was something deeply satisfying about pulling off a finicky recipe like that, especially when everything else felt so out of my control.

After I got the divinity done, I boxed up the last of the cookies for the corporate lunch, then carefully packed a small box of divinity to take to Katherine. It wasn't much, but it was something sweet to bring her, a little bit of holiday cheer to brighten up the hospital room.

Once everything was packed and ready to go, I cleaned up my space, hung my apron on its hook, and took a deep breath. It was time to head out and tackle the rest of the day—deliveries first, then a much-needed visit to see Katherine.

Chapter Fifteen

Deliveries went smoothly and didn't take much time once I got into the rhythm. It amazed me to think that I'd only started my business a few months before and to remember how much trepidation and uncertainty I'd had on those early jobs. Every task that had been a major milestone only weeks before felt like old hat at this point. Unload trays, set things up nicely, take a credit card, wish the customer luck. Just another day at the "office".

Which left me plenty of time to stop by and check in on Katherine. As I pulled into the hospital parking lot, I waffled on the box of divinity. Did Broadway stars eat sugar? I doubted it and I didn't want to see the rejection in her eyes when I handed her the box, so despite how I'd fussed with making it cutesy and appetizing, I left it on the seat as I stepped out of the van headed into the hospital. Maybe I would take it over to Ellie or Sheila later.

I made my way inside as I thought about what I would do or say if she was awake. Condolences for her sister's death were certainly in order. But now was probably not the time for any probing questions about who she thought had tried to kill her. Wandering around the small Sugar Creek hospital for a few minutes, I got completely turned around before a sweet teenage candy striper pointed me in the right direction. After asking a few different people, I was finally pointed to Katherine's room.

My stomach started to churn as I approached the door that a nurse had pointed out. What was I doing? She wasn't going to want to see me! She'd nearly been killed the day before, and her sister was dead. The door was open though, and I bit my lip and stuck my head inside, completely shocked to find Katherine standing in the middle of the room, dressed to the nines and pulling on her big hat. She whirled when she heard me enter.

"Oh, good. You're here. You're the driver, right?" She grabbed her hat and her purse and stalked out of the hospital room.

I gaped at her a moment before following her down the hall. Boy, could she move quickly. Which was surprising in the heels she wore. I jogged to catch up.

"I thought you'd be in the hospital still. I wasn't expecting to drive you anywhere. I have my catering van."

She stopped dead in her tracks and whirled on me. "Catering van?"

"I'm a caterer. I just help out my Aunt Meg with the B&B sometimes..."

I couldn't see her eyes roll because of the sunglasses, but I was sure there was a big fat eye roll directed at me.

"Sorry, I hadn't planned on driving you," I mumbled again.

Before she could decide to find herself another ride, though, a group of nurses began to approach us from the opposite hall. They giggled and held out their phones and waved at us, clearly on the prowl for selfies and autographs. Katherine growled and started walking even more quickly toward the exit. "Catering van, whatever. Just get me out of here."

The sunlight glared as I stepped out into the morning sun and I pulled on shades as I pointed out my van, all hints of early morning clouds long gone. Before we made it ten steps into the parking lot, a flurry of voices and the rapid-fire clicks of cameras surrounded us. Had the reporters followed me? Or had they been camped out at the hospital? I hadn't noticed them when I'd arrived, but I'd been pretty lost in my own thoughts, so that wasn't much of a surprise.

"Ms. Kirby! Ms. Kirby! Can you tell us what happened?"

"How are you feeling after the attack?"

"Do you know who's responsible for your sister's death?"

Katherine stopped abruptly, her entire demeanor shifting. Gone was the impatient diva. In her place stood a woman visibly shaken, vulnerability etched across her face. She turned to face the reporters, removing her sunglasses to reveal red-rimmed eyes.

"I... I'm not sure I should say anything," she began, her voice quavering. "But the public needs to know the truth."

She paused, seemingly gathering her strength. I watched, mesmerized by the transformation.

"My sister... my dear Kelly... she was murdered," Katherine's voice broke on the last word. "And I believe I was the intended target."

The reporters leaned in, hungry for more details.

"For months now, I've been terrorized by a stalker in New York. Threatening letters, suspicious packages, always feeling watched..." She shuddered visibly. "I thought coming to Sugar Creek, to my hometown, would provide an escape. But it seems this monster followed me here."

I furrowed my brow, wondering how Katherine could be so certain about this stalker theory so soon after the tragedy.

"I want justice for Kelly," she continued, a steely determination creeping into her voice. "And I want other women to be aware of the dangers out there. No one should have to live in fear like this."

As she finished, I could've sworn I saw a hint of satisfaction in her eyes, quickly masked by another wave of apparent grief.

"That's all I can say for now. Please respect my privacy during this difficult time."

With that, Katherine turned back to me, slipping her sunglasses on. "Let's go," she murmured, her voice once again dripping with impatience.

"I better not get dirty," she said under her breath as I unlocked the doors.

When we got to the van, I pulled out a rag I kept in the glove compartment and wiped down her seat and then tucked the box of divinity into the console. I knew it wasn't dirty, but I also knew she wouldn't believe that unless she saw me clean it. She hopped inside and adjusted her hat that had slid to the side and I ran around to the driver's side and jumped in, quickly starting up the engine and pulling out of the parking lot before the nurses and the reporters could see which way we'd gone.

"Back to the B&B then?" I asked as we pulled out onto the main road in front of the hospital.

"No! To the theater. They're waiting for me for rehearsal."

I chewed my lip as I craned my neck before making a turn. "Really? I thought you'd leave or at least go rest..."

"No, the show must go on." There was a fierceness in her tone and I knew that she would indeed be able to push through whatever emotions she had about the death of her sister and deliver a broadway-worthy performance. That kind of dedication was something I couldn't even imagine. I knew I would have melted down if it had been my own relation who had been killed. But to each her own, and I supposed that was one of the things that set her apart as a star, the intense dedication to the work.

"Okay, the theater, then," I replied. This whole experience was turning out to be much different from what I'd expected. I'd shown up at the hospital thinking I'd give the woman some comfort, see if I could make her more comfortable or help her back to the B&B or back to New York. But instead we were on a mission and she was as cold as ever. All grandiose visions of me being the empathetic shoulder to cry on vanished into thin air.

It made me feel very off-kilter.

After a few minutes of silence, curiosity got the best of me. "So, you have a stalker?"

Katherine's posture stiffened. "Yes," she replied, her voice dropping to a dramatic whisper. "It started three months ago, right after my last show opened on Broadway."

She launched into her account. "At first, it was just notes. Unsettling messages left in my dressing room, slipped under my apartment door. But then things got... dangerous."

I glanced at her, noting the tremor in her voice.

"One night, leaving the theater, someone tried to grab me." Katherine's knuckles whitened as she gripped her purse. "If my security hadn't been there... I don't want to think about what might have happened."

"That sounds terrifying," I murmured.

"It was," Katherine nodded. "The police were useless. Said they couldn't do anything without proof. But I knew I was in danger. The death threats started coming daily. My phone, my email, even notes tied to bricks thrown through my window."

"And you think this person followed you here?"

She nodded emphatically. "I'm certain of it. The day before... before it happened," her voice cracked perfectly on cue, "I saw someone watching the theater. A figure in a dark hoodie. When I blinked, they were gone."

As we drove through the sleepy streets of Sugar Creek, I kept glancing back at the rearview mirror, wondering if anyone was following us. What signs might I need to look for if a stalker was really out there? I didn't like it one bit. It had me feeling jittery and anxious when what I needed more than anything to get through this holiday season was calm serenity.

We pulled into the theater and surprise, surprise, more reporters waited for us, cutting our conversation short. She fluffed her hair and ran lipstick over her lips.

I'd barely been subjected to the onslaught of public attention and already I was done with it. I couldn't imagine how someone famous like Katherine put up with this day in and day out. Katherine preened for them once again and told her stalker story. It was polished, almost word for word, what she'd said earlier and that struck me as odd. But maybe it was simply her background. She was so used to putting on a performance that even this was part of the act that was Katherine Kirby.

I went in with her, this time determined to find Charles and hammer down the headcount for the party. Not to mention, I wanted to see what the mood was with the theater folk, see if I could get a clue of some kind that would help Ryan with his murder investigation, whether he wanted my help or not.

As we stepped inside, the theater was heavy with silence. Katherine stepped inside beaming, as if waiting for applause or a welcoming committee. But the lobby was empty. No eager faces, no fawning admirers—just the distant hum of rehearsals. Her lips tightened, the momentary deflation clear, but she moved to the theater doors and flung them open, head held high, like she was ready for the show to go on, whether anyone was watching or not.

Chapter Sixteen

As soon as we stepped into the theater, the energy in the room seemed to shift. The hum of rehearsals came to a total stop, and all eyes turned toward Katherine. She moved confidently down the aisle as everyone stared. I stayed near the door, watching it all unfold.

On stage, Brittney was rehearsing Katherine's part, her voice faltering as soon as she saw the star in the aisle. Her face twisted in a mix of surprise and frustration, and then she dropped the script she was holding with a loud smack against the stage floor.

"I guess that's my cue to leave," Brittney snapped, her voice tight as she stormed off the stage. The Drama Mamas, who had been sitting near the front, applauded politely as if trying to smooth over the tension, but I could see their smiles were strained, their whispers full of judgment. What were they thinking about Katherine's return, I wondered? Were they happy to have their star money maker back in the show, or were they disappointed?

Katherine paused just long enough to give Brittney a passing glance, then climbed the steps to the stage. "I'm here now," she said, loud enough for everyone to hear, like she was blessing them with her presence. "Let's get on with it, shall we?"

Her eyes swept the room, but it was Charles she was focused on. He stood off to the side, his face pulled tight, arms crossed as if he was bracing for something. For a moment, his smile flickered, replaced by something darker—anger, frustration, maybe even resentment.

"Katherine," he faintly said as he put his hands on his hips. "Glad to see you're feeling better."

"Yes, darling. It was harrowing, truly. But as you and I know, the show must go on. Kelly would have wanted it." Her voice turned down, but the sorrow didn't quite carry to her eyes. It was strange that she seemed so detached from her own sister's murder. But maybe it was her own way of dealing with the grief.

Murmurs erupted as Katherine bent and picked up Brittney's script, but Katherine paid the group no mind other than a tiny smile that played on her lips. I could tell she was enjoying the attention, and whether it was positive or negative attention didn't really matter.

"Everyone take five," Charles called out, his voice strained. "But *only* five! We'll start again from the top after a quick break."

The actors and crew dispersed, leaving an odd quiet in the room. Katherine bent over the script on the stage, but my eyes stayed on Charles. His entire body was tense, and I couldn't shake the feeling that there was more to his anger than just the stress of the show. His eyes followed Katherine, his jaw clenched, but he didn't go over and talk to her.

I waited a moment until the tension between them simmered down a bit before making my way over to him. I had to ask him about the party and despite the bad timing, I was afraid that if I didn't talk to him now, I wouldn't get the chance at all.

"Charles," I said, tapping him lightly on the shoulder. "Hi, I'm Abby Hirsch, with Deep in the Heart Catering? I'm doing the wrap party on Saturday and I was hoping we could talk about it for a moment. I still need a headcount, and we should finalize the menu."

He turned quickly, and for a moment I wasn't sure if he'd even heard me. His eyes were wild, but then he blinked as if finally seeing me. "Right," he muttered. "Look, this is really unimportant right now. Tomorrow night's opening night, and we've barely had any time to rehearse with the star of the show."

There was panic in his voice, and I took a small step back. "I get it, but I really need those numbers if you plan to have the party still," I said softly.

He ran a hand through his hair and blew out a breath. "You know, I'm thinking we might just cancel it this year. There's been too much chaos around here. Nobody is carrying their weight, there's too much stress. I might just call it all off."

My mind raced. This was not at all what I wanted. The theater party would be a major source of income, and it was very unlikely that I would be able to book something else to take its place on such short notice. I scrambled, trying to find a way to steer things in a different direction. "I know everyone's stressed and things are hard right now, but canceling the party would just add to that. They need something to look forward to. You might have a mutiny on your hands if you cancelled the party."

He let out a sharp breath and shook his head. "They don't have to know we're canceling it until after the show."

I raised an eyebrow, holding his gaze. I was grasping for straws, and it wasn't in my nature to threaten people. But desperate times and all that. "I wouldn't be able to keep that from the Drama Mamas, Charles. Ruth has been so helpful, and I'll have to let her know."

It was a threat and my cheeks burned as I said it, but I couldn't let this go. I'd already poured so much work into planning and bought some of the food, and I wasn't about to let it fall apart now. His glare flicked toward me, and for a second I thought he might explode. But then he sighed heavily, blowing out a breath like he was trying to keep it together.

"Fine," he grumbled. "But I'm not available to help you or give you numbers or whatever you need. Talk to the Drama Mamas. Let them figure it out."

He brushed past me, bumping my shoulder in a way that was just subtle enough to make me feel uncomfortable. As I watched him storm off, a chill ran down my spine. This guy was trouble. I could easily imagine him snapping at someone, maybe even worse. His anger, his bitterness—it was clear as day. But the question was, why? What could have driven him to this point? And could it really be bad enough to make him a killer?

As I turned away from Charles, my eyes landed on the Drama Mamas sitting huddled near the center of the stage and smiled. At least I wouldn't have to go hunting for someone to talk to. Approaching the row where Ruth and the other Drama Mamas sat, I could feel their eyes on me. They weren't whispering anymore, but their expressions spoke volumes.

"Hi, Ruth," I said, giving her a polite smile. "I wanted to touch base about the wrap party. Charles said to ask you about the final details." I felt bad having to ask her a second time after she'd already told me it was Charles' responsibility, but I was really stuck between a rock and a hard place.

Ruth raised her eyebrows at the women beside her before answering, her fingers absentmindedly fiddling with the edge of her notebook. "Yes, I suppose he *would* pawn that off on me." She sighed and glanced at the stage where Katherine paced back and forth, reading from the script. "What do you need to know?"

"Mostly the headcount and timing. I've already got a lot in place, but I just need to nail down a few final details."

She nodded, flipping open her notebook with slow, deliberate movements. "I think there should be around seventy-five, give or take," she said, jotting a number on the page as if to confirm it for herself. "And yes, after the show, as planned. Probably start serving the food around nine and wrap up around eleven. Maybe a little later."

Her voice was pleasant enough, but there was an edge underneath it. The other women were unusually quiet, their gazes fixed on Katherine, who was now commanding attention on stage. I glanced back toward her, noticing how easily she'd taken control of the scene. I had a feeling that was part of what was bothering them. They were used to having control and now here was this star who made everything about her.

I decided to test the waters. "Katherine seems... determined to jump right back in."

Ruth's lips tightened slightly, but her expression didn't change. "She's always been very... dedicated, even when she performed here back in high school," she replied, her tone measured. "It's one of her many strengths."

The other Drama Mamas exchanged quick glances, but no one said a word. Something was definitely off. I leaned in a little, lowering my voice. "It'll be an adjustment for everyone, with her stepping back into the lead so suddenly, I would imagine."

Ruth tilted her head, her eyes flicking to the stage where Brittney had disappeared only minutes before. "Yes, well," she began slowly, "it's always a challenge when someone... reclaims the spotlight."

The words hung in the air, just enough to suggest there was more to the story. I could feel the tension in the group, the unspoken thoughts they weren't quite ready to say out loud. Maybe they'd been hoping Brittney would get a shot at the lead after all. I didn't need to ask outright to know they weren't thrilled about Katherine's sudden return.

Ruth clicked her pen softly against her notebook. "You know how these things go. The show must go on, but it doesn't mean everyone's... on the same page."

That was the most I was going to get from her, but it was enough. I could read between the lines—the Drama Mamas had gotten used to calling the shots while Katherine was gone, and now that she was back, things were shifting in ways they didn't like.

Brittney, for one, seemed to have her own ideas about how things should have gone, and she wasn't the only one.

"Well," I said, offering Ruth a small smile, "it sounds like everything's in place for the party. I'll make sure it's something special, especially after all this."

Ruth patted my hand, her face softening a little. "I'm sure you will, hon. Let's hope it's just what we need to... smooth things over. Get this place back on the same page."

I thanked her and said my goodbyes to the women and then turned and made my way toward the back of the theater, my mind buzzing with the subtle tension I'd just uncovered. It wasn't just Katherine's return that had everyone on edge—it was the control, the power dynamics, the unspoken rivalry between the star and those who had filled her place while she was gone. And that tension was thick enough to slice through.

But who had killed Kelly? Had they actually been after Katherine? And much more importantly... would they try again?

Chapter Seventeen

Later that evening I stood at the kitchen counter at Primrose House, carefully piping dollops of goat cheese and herbs into tiny peppers for the Christmas party I was catering the next day. The smell of rosemary and toasted bread filled the room, but my mind was far from the task. I couldn't stop thinking about what I'd seen at the theater earlier—the way Brittney had stormed offstage, Charles' tension, and Katherine's almost casual attitude about everything. It didn't sit right.

I wiped my hands on my apron and paused, staring down at the neat rows of appetizers. Should I tell Ryan? He had enough on his plate without me barging in with more speculation. He'd accuse me of snooping again, and I couldn't exactly blame him. Still, something about the way everyone reacted to Katherine's return made my gut twist. Maybe it was worth mentioning... but maybe after the party.

I shook off the thought and grabbed my phone, texting Cassie. *Hey! Bonfire at Aunt Meg's tonight. Come by if you can! I could use a break, and I have stuff to share!*

I didn't elaborate, knowing she would catch my drift. I gave her maybe ten minutes before she pulled into the B&B parking lot. I smiled as I hit send, imagining Cassie's mad rush for gossip. And I wondered if she'd had any luck on her end, learning anything about the past of Katherine and Kelly and Charles.

Just as I was about to move to the next tray of appetizers, I heard the screen door creak open, followed by a gust of cold air and the unmistakable sound of Sheila Connoly's voice.

"Anybody home? I come bearing gifts!" she called, her voice carrying a hint of mischief.

I looked up from the counter, smiling as Sheila stepped inside, cheeks pink from the cold and a bottle of wine in her hand. Her grey hair was barely tamed under a knitted cap, and she was bundled in a thick scarf, looking every bit the part of a festive holiday visitor.

"Well, if it isn't the queen of Wild Hare Winery," I teased, wiping my hands on my apron as I moved toward the door. "Come on in, you're just in time for appetizers."

Sheila grinned, holding up the bottle like a trophy. "Wine and appetizers? Sounds like a perfect evening to me. How's it going in here, Miss Busy Bee?"

"Oh, you know," I said, waving a hand toward the trays of peppers and goat cheese I'd already prepped. "Just trying to stay ahead of the holiday rush. Tomorrow's party is a big one."

Sheila whistled, stepping further into the kitchen. "I don't envy you. The winery's been slammed with holiday visitors too. We've got one more day before we close up for the season, thank goodness."

I grabbed a couple of wine glasses from the cabinet. "I can imagine. People love their wine this time of year. Are you running any specials?"

"Of course," Sheila said, setting the bottle down and pulling off her scarf. "We've got tastings, gift sets, the whole nine yards. But I think everyone just wants to stock up for their holiday dinners."

I poured us each a glass and handed one to Sheila. "To surviving the holiday madness," I said, raising my glass with a grin.

"To holiday madness," she echoed, clinking her glass against mine before taking a sip. "And speaking of madness... how are things going with the starlet staying at your place? I heard Katherine's been a handful."

I sighed, taking a small sip of the wine and savoring its warmth. "She's been... interesting. Not exactly panicking over the whole situation, which I find odd. Not very broken up over her sister, either, from what I can tell. She's more focused on the show than anything else."

Sheila raised an eyebrow. "Goodness, that doesn't sound good."

"Tell me about it," I said, setting my glass down. "She seems to be more worried about how people pronounce her name than the fact that someone might be trying to kill her."

Sheila shook her head, taking another sip. "I guess that's what you get with someone like her. Always thinking about the performance."

I nodded, but my mind was still buzzing with everything that had happened earlier. I grabbed a fresh snickerdoodle from a plate on the counter and handed it to Sheila. "Here, have a cookie to go with that wine."

Sheila grinned as she took the cookie. "Now this is the kind of pairing I can get behind."

"Aunt Meg's got a bonfire going outside with Maria and her daughter. You want to go say hi?"

Sheila beamed. "Sounds perfect."

The night was cold and clear, the stars twinkling overhead as Sheila and I stepped out into the backyard. The soft glow of the bonfire greeted us, casting flickering shadows across the lawn. Aunt Meg sat in one of the Adirondack chairs, bundled in a blanket, with Maria and her daughter, Daniela, seated beside her, tending to the fire. The Japanese family that had arrived on the same day as the Kirby sisters sat across from us, toasting marshmallows and whispering quietly. The warmth of the flames was inviting, and I could smell the sweet scent of marshmallows toasting.

"Look what I brought," Sheila announced, holding up the bottle of wine as we approached. Aunt Meg's face lit up.

"Well now, this is exactly what we needed," Aunt Meg said, accepting a glass. "Maria, have a glass with us."

Maria hesitated for a moment, but then smiled. "Why not? It's been a long day."

Sheila poured generously, and I handed a mug of hot cocoa to Daniela, who sat wide-eyed and excited by the fire, spinning a marshmallow on a stick. Her dark hair was tied back in a neat ponytail, her cheeks rosy from the heat of the fire.

"Thank you, Miss Abby." She took a drink and set the mug down, her attention on the roasting puff in front of her. Christmas music drifted over the yard from a speaker on one of the picnic tables near the house, setting a festive, happy mood.

"Your bonfire idea is really something, Meg," Sheila said, settling into a chair and taking another sip of wine. "I'm thinking maybe I should do one at the winery next year."

"Oh, it's nothing fancy," Aunt Meg replied, waving a hand. "Just a bit of fire and some Christmas music to keep folks happy."

"You've certainly got the magic touch," Maria added, smiling as she took a sip of her wine. "Everyone in town seems to flock to whatever you put together."

Aunt Meg chuckled. "Well, it's Sugar Creek. Doesn't take much to draw a crowd when the weather's this cold."

I leaned back, enjoying the warmth of the fire and the company of friends. The stress of the day slowly started to melt away, though my mind still wandered now and then to everything that had happened at the theater. But here, under the stars, with a glass of wine in hand and the sound of laughter all around, it was hard to hold on to any worries.

Just as I started to relax, the sound of footsteps crunching on the gravel driveway made me look up. Cassie appeared at the edge of the yard, wrapped in a thick coat and scarf, her breath visible in the cold air.

"There she is!" I called, waving her over. "You made it!"

Cassie smiled, her eyes bright with mischief. "You didn't think I'd miss out on a bonfire, did you?"

Cassie walked over, the firelight catching in her auburn hair as she smiled at the group. She made her way to the empty seat next to me and plopped down, rubbing her hands together to warm them.

"Hey, Sheila," Cassie said, nodding toward her with a grin. "Got any of that wine left for me?"

"You know I do," Sheila replied with a laugh, already pouring a generous glass and handing it to Cassie.

Cassie took the glass with a grateful nod and settled back in her seat, taking a slow sip. "Mm, perfect. I needed this. The shop's been a madhouse with everyone trying to find last-minute Christmas gifts. You wouldn't believe how many people are looking for 'rare' antiques the week before Christmas."

"I can imagine," I said, chuckling. "You must be drowning in requests for miracle finds."

Cassie sighed dramatically. "Oh, you have no idea. People keep asking if I have a secret stash of hidden treasures in the back that I just haven't put out yet."

Sheila raised an eyebrow. "Do you?"

Cassie winked. "Wouldn't you like to know?"

We all laughed, and I felt the tension of the day slip away even further. Cassie had a way of lightening the mood, even when things were hectic. I took another sip of wine, feeling a little warmth creep into my cheeks.

"So," Cassie said, lowering her voice a little, "what's the latest on Katherine?"

Everyone leaned in as I started to tell about my day with the star.

"Well," I began, swirling the wine in my glass, "she's definitely recovered. I went to visit her at the hospital and she demanded a ride to the theater. Didn't say a peep about Kelly. She made quite an entrance, I'll say that much. Brittney was rehearsing her part, and when Katherine walked in, Brittney threw a fit. Stormed offstage in the middle of her lines."

Sheila leaned forward, eyes widening. "Wait, is she here now?" she asked, leaning toward the house and scanning the windows.

"No, she's still over at the theater as far as I know. Hasn't called for a ride, at least."

"Goodness," she replied and sank back into her chair as she took a sip of wine.

"I know, right? Lots of drama," I said, glancing at Cassie, who was listening intently. "The whole theater felt... off. Charles was tense, the Drama Mamas were whispering, and Katherine was just soaking up all the attention like she didn't have a care in the world."

Cassie frowned. "So, no one was happy to see her back?"

"Not really. At least, it didn't seem that way," I said, taking a sip of wine as I mulled over the scene. "It was strange. You'd think people would be relieved to have the star back, especially since they've all been stressing over the show, but instead, it felt like everyone was walking on eggshells."

Aunt Meg shifted in her chair, her brow furrowed in thought. "That's odd, isn't it? You'd think they'd be happy to have her back if ticket sales are up and the show is getting more attention."

"That's what I thought, too," I agreed. "But from the way Charles was acting, and the looks on everyone's faces... I don't know. It felt like they were worried about something, like Katherine's return had upset some kind of balance."

Maria nodded quietly, her eyes on the fire. "It sounds like there's more going on than just a show."

Cassie sighed, taking another sip of her wine. "Maybe it's jealousy. Brittney's been stepping in for Katherine, right? Maybe she was hoping she'd get to keep the lead."

"That crossed my mind," I said, leaning back in my chair. "But it's more than just Brittney. Charles was practically shaking, and the Drama Mamas were... well, I couldn't tell if they were relieved or annoyed. It was hard to read, but something wasn't right."

"Speaking of the Drama Mamas, they were over at the winery a little earlier," Sheila said, leaning in, her voice lowering conspiratorially. "I overheard them talking about some of this."

Aunt Meg tilted her head. "Oh? What were they saying?"

"Well, they were definitely talking about Katherine coming back, but that wasn't the only thing on their minds," Sheila continued, glancing around as if making sure no one else could hear. "It sounded like they were worried... about losing some kind of control."

I frowned, remembering what Brittney and Lisa had said about the Drama Mamas and how much control they had over things at the theater. I hadn't really thought about it before, but power and control could be a strong motivator. Could it have led them to murder, though? "Did they say anything specific?" I asked.

"I couldn't catch everything," Sheila admitted, swirling her wine thoughtfully. "But from what I overheard, they were complaining about how Charles is using Katherine's return to... I don't know, assert himself more? Like they're afraid he's going to take over more decisions now that she's in the spotlight and he can use his relationship with her as an excuse to take control."

Maria shifted in her seat, her gaze flicking to the fire. "Maybe they've been in charge unofficially for a while, and now, with Katherine and Charles working more closely, they feel like they're being pushed out."

"That makes sense," I said, thinking back to the tension I'd witnessed at the theater. "Charles was definitely acting different once Katherine stepped back on that stage today, like he's more in control. And the Drama Mamas... well, they didn't look happy about it."

Sheila leaned forward slightly, lowering her voice. "You know, the way they were talking... it almost sounded like they wanted to get rid of Charles. Not in a 'we're going to take him down' way, but more like they were brainstorming ways to keep him from getting too much power."

Cassie's eyes widened. "Get rid of him? You really think they'd go that far?"

Sheila shook her head. "I don't know if they'd actually do something drastic, but from what I overheard, they're definitely concerned about losing control. It wasn't what they said, exactly—it was more the tone. Like they were trying to figure out how to protect their position."

"So, they're not just worried about Katherine, then," I said, piecing it together. "They're worried about Charles using her to push them out."

Sheila nodded. "Exactly. And that's what has them nervous."

Aunt Meg let out a low hum, her brow furrowed in thought. "Would that have been reason enough to try to kill her, you think? Get her out of the picture?"

Maria glanced at us, her eyes dark with concern. "I don't know. That kind of fear, fear of losing power, can make people act... irrationally."

I took a slow breath, the weight of it all settling over me. The Drama Mamas might not be the innocent group of theater organizers I'd thought they were. And if they were really as upset about losing control as Sheila implied, they could become more dangerous than I'd anticipated.

Glancing at my watch, I sighed. "Well," I said, standing up and brushing off my hands, "whatever's going on, I've got a feeling it's not going to end quietly. I'm sorry, but I've got to get back to the prep work. Y'all have fun out here. I'll be home in a couple of hours, Cass."

I gave the group a small wave as I made my way back toward the house, my mind still buzzing with the pieces of the puzzle Sheila had just shared. There was more at stake than just a Christmas show. The Drama Mamas weren't just worried about the production—they were worried about losing control of something much bigger. And that made them very dangerous indeed.

Chapter Eighteen

Thursday morning I was a whirlwind of activity even before I left Cassie's house. My first big holiday catering job would be tonight and I still had cookie trays and another drop off job to worry about during the day.

The morning air was crisp as I pulled up to Primrose House, my van rumbling softly as I parked by the side. The house was unusually quiet—no sign of Aunt Meg or Katherine. Maria's car was out front, though, so I knew she was somewhere inside. I shivered as I climbed the porch steps and opened the old door, the familiar creak of the hinges echoing as I stepped into the warm entryway.

The stillness of the house was a welcome change after the hectic day before. With so much to do, the quiet felt like an invitation to focus. I headed toward the kitchen, glancing around at the tidy living room as I went. A faint hum of the vacuum drifted down from upstairs. Maria, always on top of things.

The kitchen greeted me with the lingering scent of coffee and pastries from breakfast. I placed my bag on the counter and pulled out my notebook, flipping to the page where I'd scribbled down the day's list of tasks. Tonight's party would be a big one, and I had plenty to finish up before then.

I glanced at my notes. Swedish meatballs, cranberry sauce... I had prepped most of the ingredients yesterday, but there was still plenty to do. I sketched out a quick plan for the day—finish the meatballs, simmer the sauce, box up the cookie trays for delivery—and then I got to work.

Pulling ingredients from the fridge, I set up my station and slipped into the familiar rhythm of chopping and mixing. The methodical work gave me a chance to clear my head, though the events at the theater kept creeping back in. Katherine's return had stirred up something, and not just on stage. The tension between Charles, the Drama Mamas, and everyone else was still buzzing in my mind. I tried to push it aside for now. Focus on the task at hand.

A good half-hour passed before I heard the sound of the front door opening and closing. Aunt Meg's footsteps shuffled through the hallway and into the kitchen, her cheeks flushed from the cold.

"Morning," she said, unwrapping her scarf and hanging it on the back of a chair. "Looks like you've been busy already."

"Always," I replied with a grin, stirring the pot of cranberry sauce on the stove. "How was the drive?"

Aunt Meg sighed, her expression weary. "Well, we got Katherine to the theater, but it wasn't without some drama, of course."

I raised an eyebrow. "Drama? More reporters?"

She nodded, sinking into one of the chairs at the kitchen table. "They were all over us as soon as we left the house. I had to park way around the side of the theater just to avoid the crowd. Katherine didn't say much on the way over, but I could tell she was nervous. Kept glancing out the window like she was expecting to see someone following us."

"Still worried about the stalker?" I asked, my voice lowering.

Aunt Meg shrugged. "Maybe. She didn't say anything

outright, but she's definitely on edge. I didn't see anyone suspicious, though. Just the reporters, pushing for a sound bite."

I stirred the sauce, letting the tart scent of cranberries fill the kitchen as I considered that. Katherine's stalker—if he even existed —was a mystery all on his own. But Aunt Meg was sharp. If she hadn't noticed anyone, maybe Katherine's paranoia was just that —paranoia.

"I'll bet she's playing it up for the press," I muttered, half to myself.

Aunt Meg chuckled softly. "Wouldn't surprise me. Oh, and she gave me these." She pulled two tickets from her coat pocket and laid them on the table. "For tonight's show. Opening night, you know."

I glanced at the tickets, a pang of longing hitting me. "I wish I could go, but I've got the big event tonight."

Aunt Meg nodded. "I figured. I was thinking about asking Maria to come with me instead. But we'll see."

"You should go. I bet it'll be a packed house with everything that's been going on," I said, pulling the meatballs out of the oven and setting them aside to cool. "I'm sure Katherine will be soaking up all the attention."

Aunt Meg smiled but didn't say anything. I could tell she was still thinking about the reporters and the talk about the stalker. But before we could dive into it further, I set the spoon down and turned to the cookie trays stacked by the counter.

"I've got to get these cookies boxed up and ready for delivery," I said, changing the subject. "Then I need to run to the store for a few things I'm running low on for tonight."

Aunt Meg stood and stretched, giving me a nod. "You've got a busy day ahead. I'll be upstairs if you need me. Maria's cleaning, but she'll help if you want."

"Thanks, Aunt Meg," I said, grateful for the support.

As she left the kitchen, I started boxing up the cookies, my thoughts drifting back to the theater, the reporters, and the strange energy surrounding Katherine's return. Something wasn't right, but with the day's workload, I had no time to dwell on it.

Once the cookies were packed, I grabbed my list of ingredients and slipped my phone into my pocket, mentally bracing myself for a quick stop at the grocery store. The day was only just beginning, and I had a feeling it was going to be a long one.

I packed the last tray of cookies into the back of my van and double-checked my list. Two deliveries before noon, then a quick stop at the grocery store, and I'd be ready to dive into the final prep for tonight's event. The day was moving along faster than I expected, but I could feel the pressure building. There was still so much left to do.

The first delivery was to the community center, where they were hosting a small holiday gathering. I dropped off the cookies, chatting briefly with the staff as I arranged the trays on a table near the entrance. The second delivery was to the library for a book club meeting. Both stops were quick, and I kept the conversations light, trying not to let the growing list of tasks hanging over me show.

After the second drop-off, I made my way to the grocery store. I needed to grab a few last-minute items—extra butter, parsley, cheese, and some mixed nuts. Easy enough, but even as I moved through the aisles, my mind was already racing ahead to everything I still had to finish.

By the time I reached the checkout line, the familiar feeling of unease had crept in. Not because of anything unusual, but because I still had so much left to do and not nearly enough time. The evening party was looming, and every minute felt like it was slipping away faster than I could keep up. I couldn't afford any more delays.

I loaded the groceries into the back of my van, mentally ticking off items from my to-do list as I slid into the driver's seat. There were still the final touches on the meatballs and cranberry sauce, plus boxing up more cookie trays for later deliveries. It would be close, but if I kept moving, I'd manage it.

As I pulled out of the parking lot and onto the quiet main road, I let out a breath, trying to shake off the tension. But that's when I saw it—a dark sedan, creeping along a few cars behind me. At first, I thought nothing of it. Sugar Creek wasn't a bustling city, and seeing the same car around town wasn't unusual.

But something about it nagged at me. I couldn't put my finger on why. Was I imagining things? I turned down a side street and checked the rearview mirror. The sedan was still there, keeping its distance but not turning away.

My stomach clenched. I sped up, testing it by taking another turn, weaving through a quiet neighborhood. Sure enough, the car followed.

My pulse quickened. This wasn't a coincidence.

Panic began to bubble up, and I tried to think quickly. Should I go back to Primrose House? No. Not if someone was following me. And what if Katherine's stalker was closer than we'd thought?

With my heart pounding, I made another quick decision, veering off toward the police station. The dark sedan kept pace for a moment before slowing and disappearing down a side road, vanishing from view as I pulled into the police station's parking lot.

I sat there for a few seconds, gripping the steering wheel with white knuckles, my breath shaky. Whoever had been following me was gone, but the unease lingered. It wasn't just my to-do list or the evening party anymore—something was really wrong.

I needed to talk to Ryan.

Gathering myself, I climbed out of the van and headed inside the station, feeling slightly safer now that I was here. It was time to tell Ryan everything.

CHAPTER NINETEEN

I hated to leave the groceries in the car and I hated that I was taking more time out of my already tight schedule, but I had to see if I could talk to Ryan. I knew someone had been following me, and I wouldn't feel comfortable until I told him about it.

Inside the police station, I said a quick hello to Irene before I spotted Ryan leaning over Ty's desk, looking as focused as ever, his brow furrowed as he studied some paperwork. He glanced up as I walked in, his face softening immediately.

"Hey, you," he said, his tone warm but quick, already sensing the anxiety in my expression. He stepped toward me, brushing a hand down my arm before giving me a brief but reassuring kiss. "What's wrong?"

"I think someone was following me, Ryan," I blurted out, the words tumbling out before I could stop them. "A dark sedan—it was right behind me, turning down all the same streets."

Ryan's expression shifted from warmth to concern, and he gently guided me toward his desk. "Wait, slow down. Why do you think they were following you? There aren't all that many streets to turn down around here."

I swallowed, feeling the tension in my chest. "It's not just a hunch, Ryan. It was there at every turn, and I couldn't shake it. You don't think it could be connected to Katherine's stalker, do you? Maybe they know I've been driving her around?"

Ryan frowned, his eyes narrowing in thought as he processed what I'd said. But then, instead of the urgency I'd expected, I saw something else—hesitation.

"About that stalker thing..." he said slowly. "I had another conversation with one of the investigators who was first on Katherine's case in New York. He told me he's pretty confident the whole story is made up."

"What?" I asked, taken aback. "Why would they think that?"

Ryan leaned back against his desk, folding his arms. "The investigator said they've seen this kind of thing before—people in the public eye, especially actors, sometimes report stalkers without any real evidence. It can be for attention, to gain sympathy, or as a way to manipulate people around them. Apparently, Katherine's case fits that pattern."

I stared at him, trying to process the idea. "What pattern?"

Ryan sighed. "There's no real evidence—no credible threats, no confirmed sightings, no witnesses who can corroborate what she's saying. Katherine's story just isn't adding up, and the NYPD is starting to think it's more about drama than danger."

"And you believe this guy?"

Ryan glanced out the window, considering. After a beat, he nodded.

I bit my lip, my mind racing. "But what about the car that was following me?"

Ryan let out a slow breath, reaching out to place a hand on my arm. "Abby, I know you're worried, but... it's possible that what you saw today was just a coincidence. Sugar Creek isn't exactly full of stalkers lurking in cars. And it's pretty common for people to start connecting things to fit a narrative—especially if they're hearing stories about danger. Your mind starts looking for patterns, even when there aren't any."

I pulled my arm back, frustration bubbling up inside me. "You think I'm imagining things?"

"I'm not saying that," he said quickly, his voice gentle but firm. "I just don't want you getting caught up in Katherine's paranoia. It's easy to start seeing danger when you're already on edge."

His words stung more than I wanted to admit. "I'm not paranoid, Ryan. Something is going on, and you can't just dismiss it because the NYPD doesn't think Katherine's stalker is real."

Ryan stood up, placing his hands on his hips as he met my gaze. "I'm not dismissing you, Abby. I just don't want you getting hurt or dragged into something that might not even be real. Let me handle this."

I clenched my fists, the anger simmering beneath the surface. "Fine. But don't be surprised if something happens and you realize too late that I wasn't just overreacting."

Before he could say anything else, I turned on my heel and walked out of the station, the cold air hitting me like a slap as I stepped outside. The fear that had driven me here was now mixed with frustration, and no matter how hard I tried, I couldn't shake the feeling that Ryan was wrong. Something was happening, and I wasn't about to sit back and ignore it.

I pulled my coat tighter around me, trying to shake the tension of my argument with Ryan, but the weight of his words stayed with me. The last thing I wanted was to fight with him, but I couldn't ignore the nagging feeling that he was wrong about this.

I made my way to the van, my footsteps crunching on the gravel. The van—our van, technically. Ryan had helped me pay for it when I was just starting out with the catering business. It had been a quiet gesture of support, one of the ways he'd showed me he cared, even when we weren't always on the same page. I paused as I reached the driver's side, running my fingers along the door handle.

He loved me. I knew that. And he was probably just worried about me getting hurt or involved in something I shouldn't. But it still stung.

Sliding into the driver's seat, I let out a long breath, staring at the dashboard. The tension from the conversation with Ryan was still buzzing under my skin, and my mind kept circling back to the same questions.

Was he right? Was I imagining things?

I thought about what Ryan had said, about the NYPD not believing the stalker was real, about how Katherine's story didn't add up. He was probably right in most ways—after all, the police dealt with these kinds of cases all the time. They had experience, they knew the patterns. Maybe Katherine was exaggerating, or worse, fabricating the whole thing to gain sympathy or manipulate people around her.

But still, that didn't explain what I saw today. The car had been following me. I hadn't imagined that. My heart had pounded with every turn, my instincts screaming at me to get away. That wasn't paranoia. That was real.

I stared out the windshield, watching a few people pass by on the sidewalk, bundled in coats and scarves against the cold. Maybe I was letting Katherine's drama get to me, just like Ryan had said. Maybe I was too caught up in the theater gossip, in the tension and the mystery of it all.

But that car.

I leaned my forehead on the steering wheel, replaying the moments in my head. The car had stayed with me, through every turn, every detour. It wasn't just my imagination running wild. Someone had been there, following me. And whether or not it had anything to do with Katherine's so-called stalker, I wasn't going to ignore it.

A flicker of frustration flared again, but I pushed it down. I couldn't let this consume me—not right now. I had work to do. My groceries were still sitting in the back of the van, and I only had a few hours left before I had to cater tonight's event. I glanced at the dashboard clock, my pulse quickening. I didn't have time to spiral into more questions.

Focus, Abby.

With a slow, steadying breath, I pulled my keys from my pocket and started the engine. The familiar hum of the van brought a small sense of comfort, reminding me that this was my space—my life. No matter what was happening with Katherine, with the theater, or even with Ryan, I knew what I'd seen. I wasn't about to doubt myself now.

But there would be time to sort all that out later. Right now, I had a job to finish.

I glanced at my phone, wondering if I should text Cassie or Aunt Meg, just to vent about the conversation with Ryan, but I hesitated. Maybe later. Maybe after the event was done and I could clear my head. For now, I had to shake this off and get back to work.

Because no matter what Ryan believed, I wasn't going to let this go.

I put the van into gear and pulled out of the station parking lot, my mind already shifting back to the task ahead, even if the shadow of that dark sedan still lingered in the back of my thoughts.

CHAPTER TWENTY

By the time I got back to Primrose House after leaving the police station, I was running on pure frustration. Ryan's words kept echoing in my head—his calm dismissal of what I knew I'd seen. It was infuriating, and it fueled me through the rest of the afternoon as I prepped for the catering job.

I threw myself into the work, channeling all that anger into chopping, mixing, and plating. The kitchen became a blur of activity as I moved between pots simmering on the stove and trays lined up on the counter. Swedish meatballs, cranberry sauce, potato pancakes, and other bite-sized appetizers filled the air with their savory scents, but none of it was enough to distract me from the growing knot of frustration in my chest. I didn't have time to think about stalkers, Katherine, or what Ryan had said. Not now. I had a party to cater, and the clients were counting on me.

With each task I completed, a bit of the tension eased, though it never fully let up. By the time I packed up the van and headed to the office party, I'd managed to push the whole ordeal with Ryan to the back of my mind. I needed to focus on the job ahead of me, not on the unanswered questions swirling around Katherine or the car that had followed me.

The office party was already in full swing when I arrived, with the sound of laughter and clinking glasses spilling out into the parking lot. Clearly, they'd gotten started early, and I wasted no time setting up the food station in the corner of the room as the group partied and laughed around me. The aroma of rosemary-scented potato pancakes and meatballs warming in a chafing dish quickly drew a crowd. One by one, the guests circled around, grabbing plates and showering me with compliments between bites. Conversations hummed, and I stayed on my toes, refilling trays and dishes, refreshing cranberry sauces, and making sure everything ran smoothly.

At one point, the boss—a jolly man in an ugly Christmas sweater—gave me a grateful thumbs-up and tried to talk me into joining the party. I politely declined and smiled at the good-natured chaos unfolding around me. Between off-key renditions of Christmas classics on the karaoke machine and the occasional paper hat from a party cracker landing in my direction, the event was a whirlwind of festive energy.

For a few hours, I let myself get lost in the busyness of it all. I chatted with the guests, made sure every platter stayed full. The more I threw myself into the work, the more my earlier frustrations faded into the background, at least for the moment.

But as my catering window came to a close, and I packed up everything, my mind turned back to murder and the theater.

Primrose House was dark when I arrived, a far cry from the lively atmosphere of the event. The quiet gave me too much space to think, to wonder if Ryan was right—if maybe I had been imagining things with that car. But then again, I wasn't one to let go of a gut feeling so easily.

I tossed my keys on the counter, letting the silence of the house settle around me. Everyone must be at the theater tonight, watching Katherine's big return to the stage. I hadn't seen anyone following me on the way back from the event, and as much as I kept glancing in my rearview mirror, there'd been no sign of the dark sedan following me again. Maybe I was over-thinking things, letting the theater drama creep too far into my head.

But still...

As I unloaded my things from the van, the murder of Kelly Kirby gnawed at me. Who would want her dead? Katherine had been the intended target, or at least that's what she claimed, but something didn't sit right with me. Kelly was the one who had died. But what if it was meant for Katherine? And if it was meant for Katherine, how had Kelly ended up with it? And why had Katherine been so calm afterward, as if the whole thing hadn't rattled her the way it should have?

I started the dishes in the sink as my mind turned and turned, working through the possibilities. Maybe it wasn't about Katherine's fame at all. Maybe Kelly had known something she shouldn't have. Or maybe this was all just a convenient smokescreen to cover up something else. But what?

Everyone was at the theater tonight—Charles, the Drama Mamas, Brittney—and all of them seemed to have something to hide. If someone had wanted Kelly dead, then the clues were in that building. I just had to figure out who was pulling the strings and why.

After unloading the last of the trays into the sink, I glanced at a note Aunt Meg had left on the counter.

"Took everyone to the theater for the show! See you soon! - Aunt Meg"

Of course, everyone was there, watching the performance. Maybe Katherine had managed to captivate the crowd with her star power, but I couldn't stop wondering what else was playing out behind the scenes. Was she covering for someone? Was Charles in over his head with all this? And what about the Drama Mamas, always so quick to jump in and control everything?

The questions circled in my mind, but without answers, they only added to the growing sense of unease. No matter how much I scrubbed or cleaned, I couldn't shake the feeling that something was about to break. And when it did, I had to be ready.

With a sigh, I turned my focus to the dishes, scrubbing away the remnants of the evening's chaos. My mind was still buzzing with questions I couldn't answer, but I tried to focus on the simple task in front of me. At least this was something I could control.

The sound of car doors and chatter outside broke through my thoughts a little while later. Aunt Meg was back.

I dried my hands quickly just as the front door opened. Laughter and footsteps echoed down the hall, and soon Aunt Meg breezed into the kitchen, her face lit up with excitement.

"Oh, Abby! You missed quite a show," she said, her eyes bright as she unwrapped her scarf.

I smiled, stepping over to give her a quick hug. "That good, huh?"

"It was incredible," Aunt Meg gushed. "That Katherine, she's something else. I can see why she's such a star on Broadway. The way she commanded the stage... it was like she was born for it. Hard to believe she was in the hospital just yesterday, and lost her sister...she covered it all up really well."

I nodded. "That's what I saw too, when I picked her up from the hospital yesterday. She seems to be really good at shutting off those emotions. Is it an act, though? I can't tell."

Aunt Meg shrugged. "It's hard to know what anyone else is thinking, especially when it comes to grief." Her voice was quiet, and I wondered if she was thinking back to losing her husband, my Uncle Nolan. I felt bad for bringing sad things to mind.

"Tell me more about the theater," I asked her, hoping to steer the conversation in a different direction.

As Aunt Meg regaled me with highlights from the performance, I found myself both intrigued and a little disappointed I'd missed it. I turned back to the sink, fishing out a whisk and running it under the hot water.

"The costumes were spectacular too," Aunt Meg continued.

"And the set design! You wouldn't believe what they managed to do with our little stage."

"Sounds amazing," I said, a twinge of regret in my voice. "I wish I could've made it."

"Where is the star now? Did you give her a ride home?"

"No, she said she would get a ride home with someone from the theater."

It was strange, given how adamant she'd been about having car service and holding herself at a distance from the others at the theater. The things Ryan had said about her faking the stalker bounced around in my mind. Would she have stayed behind if she was really worried about a stalker? But I shrugged the thoughts off. The hurt from Ryan's not believing me was too fresh, and I didn't want to think in that direction.

"Well, enough about the show," Aunt Meg said, waving a hand. "How was your event, honey? You've been busy all evening! And here I am, bragging about the fun I've had."

I couldn't help but smile, remembering the antics of the office party. "It was great, actually. Really fun group. They insisted I join in for a round of karaoke."

Aunt Meg's eyebrows shot up. "You didn't!"

I laughed, shaking my head. "Don't worry, I politely declined. But the food was a hit. They practically licked the platters clean."

"That's wonderful, honey," Aunt Meg beamed, patting my arm. "I'm so proud of you, you know. Building this business of yours."

Her words warmed me, chasing away the small disappointment of missing the show. "Thank you. It's not always easy, but it's getting better and better all the time. I couldn't do it without your help though, that's for sure. That and your kitchen," I added with a laugh.

Aunt Meg squeezed my shoulders and moved to make herself a cup of tea. "So, what's on the agenda for tomorrow? You've got that baby shower to cater, right?"

I nodded. "Yeah, Ellie's baby shower in the evening. It's going to be a pretty big one, so I'll be tied up with that all day. I just hope I don't run out of time with all the prep work."

Aunt Meg smiled knowingly. "You'll do fine, Abby. You always do. And I'm going all out on the bonfire for the community tomorrow night. I've got half the town talking about it."

I let out a small sigh. "I wish I could be there."

"Don't you worry about it," Aunt Meg said, giving me a reassuring smile. "I've got everything under control. You focus on your catering. We'll save a s'more for you."

I smiled, appreciating her optimism, though the thought of missing out still stung. "Thanks, Aunt Meg. I'll try to wrap up early, but you know how these things go."

She nodded and grabbed her cup of tea from the microwave, stretching a little as she prepared to head to bed. "Well, I'm off to get some sleep. Tomorrow's going to be a big day. Sleep tight and we'll see you bright and early, I'm sure."

"You know it. Goodnight, Aunt Meg," I said softly, watching her head toward the stairs.

Once the house quieted down again, I finished tidying up the last of the dishes, but my thoughts kept drifting back to the play—and to Katherine. How did she manage to dazzle the crowd after everything that had happened to her? And who had killed Kelly? Nothing added up, and the more I thought about it, the more it all gnawed at me. Not to mention the possibility that the car had been following me after all.

Something wasn't right. I just had to figure out what it was.

Chapter Twenty-One

"There she is," Aunt Meg said with a smile as I breezed through the side kitchen door a little after eight the next morning. She was standing at the kitchen counter in my apron, whipping something into a frenzy with an outrageous amount of force.

I laughed. "What are you doing over there?"

She stopped the mixer and pulled a spoon out of the drawer, then stuck it into the bowl. "Whipped cream. An overwhelming desire for pumpkin pie took over me when I woke up this morning and I couldn't resist."

I raised my eyebrows. "Uh, wrong holiday," I said as I licked the spoon. "But delicious nonetheless." It was creamy and smooth with a hint of vanilla and cinnamon. I wanted to swirl about a gallon of it into my coffee.

She shrugged. "The stomach wants what the stomach wants. Besides, the family who's staying with us is from Japan, so I doubt they'll know this isn't traditionally a Christmas dessert."

I glanced around the kitchen and at Aunt Meg baking, feeling a sudden wave of nostalgia. Memories of countless mornings spent baking together rushed back, the rhythm of mixing, the warmth of the oven, the shared laughter. I leaned in and gave her a quick squeeze, and she laughed as whipped cream splattered us both.

"Sorry," I said, grinning as I wiped off a stray dollop of cream. The scent of spices and sugar filled the kitchen, making my stomach grumble.

"What have you got going on today?" I asked as I moved to the pantry to take stock of our staple goods. My hunch that the sugar was getting low was correct, and I added it to the running grocery list on my phone.

"The usual for the most part," she said as she poured herself a cup of coffee and added a generous dollop of whipped cream on top. I grinned and did the same. "But Maria and I are going to set things up for the bonfire too. She had some ideas for festive appetizers for the happy hour."

I took a sip of the coffee, savoring the warmth and the holiday flavors. "Do y'all need help? I could probably do a few trays of cookies in between the stuff for Ellie's party."

She waved my comment away. "No worries, we have it under control!"

Maria came in just then and interrupted our conversation. "Good morning!" she said as she hung her purse in the closet. "It smells delicious in here."

Aunt Meg had just opened the oven door and was sliding out a perfectly baked pumpkin pie.

"Oh, pie! That's what it is!" Maria waggled her eyebrows up and down. "Do we get a piece?"

"You better believe it," Aunt Meg told her and set the pie on a cooling rack. "This baby is for us first. If there's any leftover, we can offer it to guests."

I watched them happy in the kitchen and wondered if I should spoil the mood by talking about the drama with Katherine and the car that had followed me the day before. I hesitated, my mind flashing back to the car. I'd been debating whether to tell Aunt Meg and Maria about it ever since, but I hadn't mentioned it yet.

What would I say? And besides, I didn't want to worry them if it really was nothing. I hadn't seen anything suspicious since, and Ryan had been so sure that I was overreacting. Maybe he was right. Maybe I was letting all of Katherine's drama cloud my judgment.

But still... I knew what I saw.

I glanced at Aunt Meg, busy with her pie, and Maria setting out plates. They looked so relaxed, so at ease. There was no point in worrying them over something I wasn't even sure about. I'd already talked to Ryan, and he didn't seem concerned. If anything really was going on, he'd handle it.

I took a deep breath, pushing the thoughts away. "I've got to get started on the bacon-wrapped dates," I said, turning back to the counter and pulling out the ingredients. It was easier to focus on work than to dwell on something I couldn't change.

As I laid out the dates and started filling them with goat cheese and then wrapping them in bacon, Maria and Aunt Meg sliced up the pie, offering me a piece.

"Not right now," I sighed, waving my bacon-greased hands in their direction with a laugh. "But save me a piece of that for later, alright?"

Before I had time to put the dates into the oven, Ryan stepped into the kitchen and I stopped dead in my tracks. I was always happy to see him, even despite my mixed feelings about our conversation the day before. But having him drop into Primrose House unannounced was very out of character and the look on his face told me that something was very wrong.

"I'm sorry to surprise y'all, but I need to speak with Katherine Kirby. Is she here?"

Aunt Meg nodded and wiped her hands on a towel. "She's still in her room, as far as I know," she told him. "What's going on?"

"We've had another murder over at the theater," he said. Aunt Meg grabbed the closest chair and slid down into it, her hand over her mouth. I met his gaze, and I sighed, sadness shrouding me.

"Who?"

"Charles Dunhill. The cleaning crew found him early this morning. Looks like he died last night..." he hesitated and glanced at me a long moment before continuing, "in the same way that Kelly Kirby died."

"Poison?" I whispered.

He nodded. "In a bottle of champagne. I'd like to speak with Ms. Kirby about last night. Do you mind telling me which room she's staying in?"

Aunt Meg's face paled, and she put a hand to her mouth a moment before answering. "This is getting out of hand. Charles was—he was just at the play last night."

I met Ryan's gaze, trying to wrap my head around it. Charles was dead? My stomach turned, a wave of sadness shrouding over me. "Does this have to do with Kelly?" I asked, my voice barely above a whisper. "Does this mean Charles didn't...?"

Ryan didn't respond, but the sadness in his eyes said it all. Whatever suspicions there had been about Charles, they were irrelevant now.

Aunt Meg hopped up and motioned for him to follow her. He threw one last look at me, his eyes sad and tired, and my heart went out to him. So much for a quiet Christmas in Sugar Creek.

I turned back to the counter and finished wrapping bacon around the dates I'd stuffed earlier. The work gave me something to focus on, something to keep me grounded as my thoughts spiraled. If Charles was dead, and in the same way that Kelly had died just days before, did that mean that Charles was innocent of Kelly's murder? It seemed likely. But if that was true, then who was responsible for both of their deaths?

The stalker theory made less and less sense. What motive could a stalker have for killing Charles? It didn't fit. If there was a connection, it had to be something deeper—something that tied back to the theater, or to the people involved.

So then, the likely culprit was probably someone from Sugar

Creek. It seemed to make sense that it would be someone who had known them all in the past.

All of this speculation hurt my head, though. I couldn't seem to make sense of anything anymore. What I wanted was to talk to Cassie about it all, get her opinion. Maybe between the two of us, we could figure something out. I cleaned my hands and pulled out my phone to text her.

"There's been another murder. Can you talk?"

She responded after a minute. *"On my way."*

I blew out a breath and tried to call her. I hadn't meant for her to drop everything and run over. But she didn't answer, so I decided to roll with it. Maybe she could give me her opinion of the stuffed dates while she was here.

Cassie flung open the door a few minutes later, surprising me so much I almost dropped the tray of dates I'd just pulled out of the oven.

"What's going on?" she asked, her face full of emotion—both excitement and sadness at war within her. She dropped her purse onto the counter and pulled off her coat, her eyes already searching mine for an explanation.

Cassie's eyes widened when I told her about Charles, and she hopped up on a barstool. "Well, that changes everything," she said as she fiddled with her key ring.

"I know, right? It makes the stalker scenario suspect, at the very least. Why would Katherine's stalker kill Charles?" I asked. As I said it, I realized that between my visit to Ryan and the hectic party I'd catered, I hadn't had a chance to tell her about my possible run-in with being followed the day before. "Speaking of the stalker, I think I was followed around town yesterday, but Ryan thinks it's all a hoax."

Cassie's eyes widened in shock as I gave her the details of both the car following me and Ryan's reaction and his theory about the stalker angle being a hoax.

"Whoa, that really complicates everything. I mean, obviously somebody was following you. But why?" she asked. "And Ryan should know better," she threw in with a frown.

I loved that she believed me outright, unlike my boyfriend, who was too quick to decide it was all in my head.

"I know, right? I have no idea why anybody would be following me. But with this thing with Charles...I don't know. Maybe the stalker thing really is a hoax. There's no motive for a stalker to go after the theater manager."

"You're probably right. That doesn't make sense. But it's weird that you were followed. Could it have been for some other reason?"

I wracked my brains as I placed the dates in a chafing dish and covered it with plastic wrap. "I don't know. But maybe we should mark the stalker possibility off our list? What do you think?"

I frowned as I put a date on a plate and handed it over.

I watched her face and pondered what she said as she took a delicate bite. She closed her eyes and smiled, a good sign. "Nice," she said after a minute and made a pouty face. I laughed and handed her another one.

"Here's the problem with getting rid of the stalker completely. We don't know if the murders were committed by the same person. We're just guessing about that," she said.

It was a good point. There was some possibility that there was more than one murderer out there. But that seemed very unlikely, given the circumstances.

"You think Ryan's getting anything juicy from the star?" Cassie said as she licked her fingers.

I shrugged and finished with the dates, then quickly washed the pan.

Cassie raised an eyebrow. "There's only one way to find out." She slid off the barstool, a mischievous glint in her eye.

"Cassie, no," I warned, already knowing what she was planning.

"Oh, come on! We could just eavesdrop a little, see if we can catch anything."

I hesitated, glancing toward the kitchen door. The idea of eavesdropping was tempting—too tempting, actually. What could Katherine possibly be telling Ryan right now? But I knew it wasn't a good idea.

"Fine," I muttered, giving in. "But we're just listening. If we don't hear anything, we're done."

Cassie grinned and grabbed my arm, pulling me toward the stairs. We crept to the bottom, straining to hear any sign of the conversation happening above us. But there was nothing—just muffled voices that we couldn't make out.

After a few minutes, I gave Cassie a look. "I told you, we're too far away to hear anything."

She sighed, disappointed. "I guess you're right, dang. But I still think Katherine knows more than she's letting on."

I nodded in agreement. "So do I."

We went back to the kitchen, and I looked around, trying to figure out what to work on next, but I was flustered by everything that was going on and had a hard time concentrating.

"You know what we should do?" Cassie said as my eyes wandered over the mess I'd already made.

I shook my head. There was no way. "Nope. Not doing anything! I have Ellie's shower tonight. I need to focus."

"Come on, you look like you could use a break! We could just drop by the theater for a few minutes..."

"What about the shop? Don't you have work to do?"

"I got Mandy to watch it."

"Well, I can't leave! I'm in the middle of cooking for Ellie's party. Why don't we wait and talk to Ryan, see if he's got any more information he can share..."

She cut me off with an eye roll. "Oh, yeah, Mr. Stay-out-of-my-investigation-you're-hallucinating is gonna share more information with us." Blowing out a breath, she leaned on the counter.

"Come on, Abby. Look at you, you've been on your feet too long. I can tell by that slouch in your back. Besides, you've probably planned this shower thing to within an inch of its life. I bet you've got at least an extra hour or two of wiggle room. Let's go see what us girls can find out."

It really made me mad that she was right. "Fine. But only an hour. I'm not kidding. And if I botch this party, I'm blaming it all on you."

She bounced around and stuck another date in her mouth. I grabbed the tray and stuck the appetizers quickly into a final container, then popped it into the fridge before running out the kitchen door with her, knowing that I would probably regret what we were about to do.

CHAPTER TWENTY-TWO

Cassie's truck rumbled down Main Street as we cruised through town toward the theater. The cold December air seeped through the windows, even with the heat blasting, but I didn't mind. It felt good to be out, even though I wasn't entirely sure what we were going to find at the theater.

"So, who should we talk to when we get there?" Cassie asked as she focused on the road. "Do you know anybody?"

I frowned. "Maybe Lisa, the costume designer? She's always hanging around backstage. But I don't know if she'd know anything. Or we could try talking to Brittney again."

She tapped her fingers against the steering wheel, thinking. "Do you think Brittney would talk to us again? I mean, if she had anything to do with Charles' death, wouldn't she try to avoid us?"

I shrugged. "Maybe, but it doesn't make sense for Brittney to kill him if they were romantically involved. He was her ticket out of here, right? Why would she throw that away?"

"I don't know. That's a really good question."

I sighed, staring out the window as we passed the town square, which was twinkling with Christmas lights. "It doesn't make sense.

None of it does. Why would she kill someone she was involved with, especially if he could help her career?"

Cassie drummed her fingers on the steering wheel again, then suddenly perked up, her eyes wide with excitement. "Hey, what if the champagne wasn't meant for Charles? What if it was meant for Katherine again, like before?"

I blinked, turning the idea over in my mind. "You think so?"

Cassie nodded eagerly. "Think about it. What if Charles wasn't supposed to die at all? What if both of them—Kelly and Charles—died by accident because the poison was meant for Katherine?"

"That would be tragic," I said, feeling the weight of the idea. "But I guess it's possible. It would explain why it doesn't make sense for someone to kill Charles."

Cassie bit her lip, her enthusiasm fading a little. "Still, that would mean someone's been targeting Katherine from the start. If the stalker isn't real, like Ryan thinks, then who else would have a reason to go after her?"

I shook my head, feeling the questions pile up again. "I don't know. Maybe someone from her past, someone we haven't thought of yet."

Cassie mulled it over for a minute, then asked, "Do you think those Drama Mamas you've been telling me about would talk to us? They always seem to be in the middle of everything."

"Probably. They seemed nice enough. Let's start there, at least, see if we can make any progress."

I giggled as we cruised by the police station, noticing that Cassie had slowed down and was craning her neck toward the building.

"Trying to catch a glimpse of Mr. Fiancé?" I teased, giving her a nudge.

Cassie laughed, her face turning a little pink. "I wasn't! Well, maybe a little," she admitted, a grin breaking through. But then her expression turned serious. "He wouldn't like this. Ryan wouldn't either. You don't think he's over there at the theater right now do you? Investigating or something? That would be bad."

I sighed, glancing back at the police station as we passed. "He might be, but I doubt it. It's already been a few hours since it happened. Besides, we're not doing anything wrong... yet."

Cassie shot me a sideways glance. "Yet. I like the sound of that. We're just a couple of concerned citizens, right?"

"Exactly," I said, a small smile tugging at my lips, though I couldn't shake the nervous flutter in my stomach. We weren't exactly going to play by the rules tonight, but I was hoping that whatever we found at the theater would help us make sense of the chaos surrounding us.

My heart flip-flopped as we pulled into the nearly empty parking lot. I couldn't believe I'd let Cassie talk me into this when I had an event pressing down on me in just a few hours.

"Seriously, Cassie. Just a few minutes, then we're out of here."

Cassie grinned and did a little hop as we walked toward the entrance, and I sighed. "I'll help you when we get back, I promise! Just give me an apron and call me an employee!"

I rolled my eyes. "That doesn't make it any better."

The theater loomed ahead, quiet and unassuming, but there was something off. As soon as we stepped inside, I noticed the difference—the lights were dim, and there was none of the usual hustle and bustle I'd come to expect.

Frowning, I stuck my head in the door to the main theater, glancing around the vast space. The stage was empty, the chairs abandoned, and only a single spotlight shone down from above, casting an eerie glow across the stage.

"Huh," I said to Cassie. "I don't know where everybody is. I thought they'd all be here for some reason. Although I suppose with Charles gone..."

Cassie shifted nervously beside me. "This place feels weird, doesn't it? Like... too quiet."

I nodded, the unsettling vibe gnawing at my gut. The whole theater felt like it was holding its breath, waiting for something.

We wandered further into the building, heading toward the front rows of the auditorium. And then we spotted them—the Drama Mamas, huddled together in the front row, their heads bent close as they whispered amongst themselves.

"There they are," I whispered, nudging Cassie.

The women looked tense, their expressions grim, and for a moment, I wondered if this was a good idea. But Cassie was already walking ahead, her shoulders back and her confidence unwavering. I followed her lead, even though my stomach felt like it was doing somersaults.

"Excuse me, Ruth?" I said as we approached the group, my voice quiet but firm. The women turned to look at us, their expressions a mix of surprise and suspicion. "I was wondering if we could ask you a few questions?"

Recognition flickered in Ruth's eyes as she looked at me. "Oh, right. The caterer." She turned to the others. "This is the girl who was supposed to cater the wrap party. I'm sorry, but I don't think that's going to happen now."

My heart sank. So it was true—no wrap party. Not that I should have expected otherwise, but hearing it confirmed still stung. All that work, all the time I'd invested in preparing for the event, gone in an instant.

But I couldn't dwell on that right now. I had bigger questions to ask.

"I'm sorry to hear that," I began. "But we were just coming by to check on y'all after everything that's happened."

The women exchanged glances, a silent communication passing between them.

"Well, isn't that sweet," one of the women drawled, her tone suggesting it was anything but. "We're just peachy, thanks for asking."

Cassie and I exchanged glances. These women didn't seem like they wanted to share anything. But then another one piped up.

"It's a terrible thing that happened to Charles," she said, shaking her head, though her expression didn't quite match her words.

Ruth shrugged. "Yes, so sad. But these things happen."

"Are you planning on cancelling the show, then?" I asked.

"Oh, no. Absolutely not. We only have two nights left and both of them are sold out already. It's unheard of for our little theater. We are definitely not cancelling."

"But surely Charles' loss will impact the production?" Cassie prodded.

One of the women let out a bark of laughter. "Oh, honey. We've been running this theater since before you were in diapers. Long before Charles came along, and we'll keep it going long after."

"Truth be told," another one leaned in, a mischievous glint in her eye, "things might run a bit smoother without all the... drama Charles brought to every rehearsal."

"Ladies!" Ruth admonished, but then she smirked. "Though I can't say I'll miss his 3AM phone calls about 'urgent' lighting changes."

"Or his insistence on that awful interpretive dance number in last year's 'A Christmas Carol'," another one added with an eye roll.

"Scrooge doing the moonwalk," the other one shuddered. "I still have nightmares."

The women cackled, momentarily forgetting we were there. It was clear they didn't think much of Charles, but that didn't necessarily make them killers.

"But... don't you need a director?" I asked, bewildered by their cavalier attitude.

Ruth waved a hand dismissively. "Please. Between the lot of us, we have over a century of theater experience. We'll manage just fine."

Cassie, never one to beat around the bush, suddenly asked, "Do any of you have any ideas who might have been behind the murders?"

The Drama Mamas exchanged startled glances before one of them quipped, "Maybe Charles killed Kelly and then offed himself when he realized what a terrible director he was."

"Barbara!" Ruth exclaimed, swatting her arm.

Barbara had the grace to look sheepish. "Sorry, not something to kid about, I know."

Another one of them cleared her throat. "In all seriousness, we've been wracking our brains about it. It's just so... bizarre."

"Well," I ventured, "Katherine mentioned she thought she had a stalker. Do you think that could be what's going on?"

"Seems a bit convenient, if you ask me," Barbara muttered.

"It's possible, I suppose," Barbara conceded. "But why would a stalker kill Charles? And why here in Sugar Creek?"

Ruth nodded. "If you want my opinion, I think it might be someone local. Someone who knew both Katherine and Charles."

"But who would want to hurt them both?" Cassie asked.

The women fell silent, each lost in thought. Ruth was the first to speak again, shifting the conversation.

"You know," she said, "we always give the house manager a bottle of champagne on opening night. It's been a tradition for more than thirty years."

Cassie and I exchanged another look, our minds clearly going in the same direction. Before either of us could speak, Ruth waved a hand. "I know what you're thinking, but trust me, honey, we had nothing to do with Charles' murder."

She must have seen the skepticism in my eyes because she pressed on. "Look, the show's been a raging success. Tickets are sold out, the cast is happy, and we've got two more nights left.

Why on earth would we want to stir up this kind of chaos now? We wanted to finish strong, not deal with a scandal."

"But who brought the champagne to Charles?" I asked.

The women exchanged glances again, this time more uncertain. "I had one of the stagehands take it over to his room before the show started," Ruth said.

"So many people could have touched it. Not to mention, it's been a tradition here for more than thirty years. So anyone who's been through the theater system would know about the champagne bottle. I'm sure it was sitting unattended in his dressing room for most of the show."

"It's hard to believe that he's gone though. Am I right, ladies? Charles has been a part of the theater since he was a kid," another of them said.

The group grew sober then, all of them lost in thoughts and memories.

"You remember back when it was him, Katherine, Trent, and Kelly running around like they owned the place? They called themselves the 'Rat Pack'—always causing a fuss."

"Trent?" Cassie asked, raising an eyebrow.

"Yeah, Trent," Ruth replied. "He used to hang out with them all the time. A little odd, but he was loyal to Charles and Katherine. The group of them were inseparable back then."

"And Kelly?" I prompted.

Margaret let out a long breath. "Oh, those two sisters... always at each other's throats. I don't know if it was jealousy, or just that they were too much alike. Either way, it was constant—over boys, parts in the shows, anything you can think of."

"Doesn't surprise me," Barbara added. "Kelly hated living in Katherine's shadow, but Katherine... well, she's always been a bit of a diva. Even back then."

Ruth nodded thoughtfully. "Still, whatever tension there was between the sisters, I can't see how it would lead to this. Something doesn't add up, not with Kelly dead and now Charles too."

We sat in silence for a moment, the laughter from earlier fading into an uneasy quiet.

I had another thought. "Was Charles the one who contacted Katherine to come to town for the show? Or was it someone else?"

She laughed. "Oh, no. Being in the show was all Katherine's idea. She's the one who called Charles to suggest it. Well, you can just imagine how shocked he was. But of course he said yes, how could he refuse? A big Broadway star in our little Christmas play! We couldn't be luckier."

What? This entire time, I'd assumed that Katherine had agreed to do the show as a favor. But the opposite was true. Why would she do it? She seemed to not enjoy being back in Sugar Creek, so I doubted it was nostalgia that had motivated her. Things didn't add up with Katherine. It made no sense, but no matter how much I tried to figure it out, my mind couldn't make sense of it all.

Barbara snorted. "Luckier? Only if 'lucky' means Charles staying up all night, micromanaging every tiny detail. If Katherine knew what she'd signed up for, she'd have run the other way!"

As the women dissolved into laughter again, I felt even more that we were missing something important. But what?

Glancing at my watch, my heart jumped into my throat. We'd spent way too much time poking around in things that were not our business while my own business was being sorely neglected. But I couldn't leave without trying to convince them to change their mind about the party. I needed that job, and I needed it bad.

I cleared my throat softly, glancing at Ruth. "Listen, I know this is all... overwhelming. But I just wanted to say, maybe cancelling the wrap party isn't the best idea."

Barbara scoffed. "Are you kidding? Charles is dead. Do you really think people are in the mood for a party right now?"

"I know, I know," I said quickly, holding up my hands to keep her from shutting me down completely. "But hear me out. Sometimes, people need something to hold on to. They need a little normalcy, especially after something like this. The cast and crew—

they've worked so hard. And with everything happening, maybe this party could help remind them why they love doing this in the first place."

Ruth exchanged a glance with the other women. They weren't sold, not yet. I pressed on, my voice softening.

"It's not just about the show, it's about the community. I think, after losing Charles, people are going to need to come together. And this could be a way to honor him, too—to celebrate the work he put into this production."

Another woman sighed, her shoulders slumping slightly. "I don't know, it seems disrespectful...and it seems like a lot of hassle."

I leaned in a little, looking at Ruth, hoping she'd understand. "I'll make sure everything runs smoothly. I can keep it respectful, a celebration of the theater more than a party. We can still do this for everyone who's worked so hard. What do you say?"

Ruth frowned, clearly torn. Finally, she let out a long breath. "Maybe you're right. Maybe it's better to keep things as normal as possible, given the circumstances."

Barbara crossed her arms but didn't argue. "I suppose if Ruth's on board, we can give it a try. But don't expect people to be in a party mood."

The rest of them nodded their heads, and I grinned.

"Understood," I said, relief flooding me. "I promise, we'll keep it low-key and appropriate. Thank you."

Ruth gave me a small nod. "Alright, Abby. Go ahead with your plans. We'll have the wrap party, but let's just make sure it's more of a quiet gathering, okay?"

"Absolutely," I agreed quickly, eager to wrap things up before anyone could change their mind. "Okay, well, thank you, ladies! Nice to meet you all! Time for us to go!" I tugged at Cassie and the two of us hustled out of the theater.

Chapter Twenty-Three

"I liked them!" Cassie said, trying to keep up with my quick pace as we jogged to the truck. "Interesting characters, don't you think?"

"They certainly are," I replied, glancing at my watch and nearly having a conniption. My stomach flipped when I realized we'd been at the theater for almost an hour. Panic started to rise in my chest. If I didn't get back to Primrose House soon, Ellie's baby shower might turn into a disaster. As long as I didn't have any more interruptions, I could pull it off—but given how the day had gone so far, I wasn't holding my breath.

Cassie revved up the engine and headed down the road. "Doesn't seem like the Drama Mamas had anything to do with Charles' murder, though. They're probably just relieved the show is almost over."

I nodded. "Yeah, I got the same feeling. They might be a little too happy about it, but it doesn't seem like they'd risk derailing the whole production when they're so close to being done."

Cassie glanced over at me. "But what about Brittney? I don't see any reason to rule her out yet. I mean, maybe the champagne was meant for Katherine, not Charles. Could it have been an accident?"

I chewed on my lip. "It's possible. But I would think Brittney would've known the champagne was meant for Charles, right? So if she was trying to poison Katherine, why use the bottle meant for someone else?"

Cassie frowned. "True. But maybe she didn't care who it hit, as long as it caused enough drama."

"I don't know, doesn't seem like her," I muttered, the weight of it settling on me. "Brittney's ambitious, sure, but poisoning someone seems extreme, especially if she's doing it without much control."

"So, if it's not the Drama Mamas, and it might not be Brittney, who else do we have?" Cassie asked, glancing out the window as the streets of Sugar Creek rolled by.

I paused for a moment, thinking. "What about this Trent guy that Ruth mentioned? We don't know him, but if he was close with Katherine and Charles back in the day, maybe he's involved in some way. Could he be the stalker?"

Cassie's eyes widened. "That's an interesting thought. We should try to look him up, see if he's still living in town or if anyone's heard from him recently. If he's part of this, we need to know where he fits in."

I agreed. "Definitely. He seems like someone we can't ignore, especially with all these strange connections."

We pulled up to Primrose House, the soft glow of Christmas lights welcoming us back. Cassie turned off the engine and turned to me. "You need help getting everything ready for the baby shower?"

I shook my head. "No, I've got it under control. At least, I hope I do. But thanks for offering."

Cassie grinned, giving my shoulder a playful shove. "I'll swing by Ellie's place early and help you set up, okay? You've got enough on your plate."

I smiled gratefully. "Deal. I'll see you in a bit."

Without wasting another second, I hopped out of the truck and raced inside, the weight of everything I still had to do pressing down on me. Time to get to work. I didn't have a second to spare if I wanted to pull this off.

————

By the time I returned to the kitchen, the flustered energy from earlier still buzzed in my veins. There was so much left to do, and every second I'd spent away from the prep felt like it had added another brick to the growing wall of stress. But this was my job, and no matter how much chaos surrounded me, I had to pull it together. I took a deep breath, letting the familiar scents of the kitchen—spices, sugar, and bacon—calm my racing thoughts. I rolled up my sleeves, ready to dive back into work, and glanced at my prep list.

Relief flooded me when I remembered that the divinity was already done. At least that was one less thing to worry about. That gave me one win, and I was grateful for it. But there was still so much left to do.

Savory options included chicken and waffle skewers with maple butter, cranberry pecan chicken salad in puff pastry cups, a pear and brie salad, and the bacon-wrapped dates. With less than two hours to prep and load the van, I couldn't afford to slow down now.

As I moved to pull the puff pastry sheets out of the fridge, Aunt Meg popped her head into the kitchen, her face flushed with excitement from whatever task she'd been working on outside.

"I know you're busy with a million things right now, and so am I, but when you have some free time, I'd love to talk about Christmas dinner," she said, a little breathless.

I raised an eyebrow, but smiled. "You're right about the million things part. But go ahead, what's up?"

"The Nagasaki family is leaving tomorrow, so other than Katherine, we'll have the place to ourselves," she continued, sounding hopeful. "And who knows, Katherine might not stick around either. I've already invited Maria and Daniela to join us, and Ryan, of course. It'll be a small affair this year, but I want to make it really special, you know?"

I nodded, pulling out a cutting board and grabbing a sack of local pecans to chop for the cranberry salad. "Is Bertie coming?"

Aunt Meg shook her head. "I don't think so, not this time. Her son invited her to visit him, so I think she's going to do that."

"Darn. Oh, well." I chopped the pecans, watching them fall into a neat pile as I thought about how different this Christmas would be. "Yeah, it would be nice to do something special. A roast at the very least, some pies maybe. Do you have any thoughts? Other than pumpkin pie?" I teased, glancing up at her with a smirk.

Aunt Meg swatted at my backside with a kitchen towel, laughing. "Oh, hush! I do love my pumpkin pie, but I'll leave the rest up to you, Miss Fancy Caterer."

We both chuckled, the moment of lightness breaking through the tension that had been hanging in the air since the news of Charles' death. It felt good to laugh, even if just for a moment.

"Alright, well, you know I'm game for whatever you want," I said, returning my focus to the pecans. "I'll think up a few ideas and we can go over them tomorrow."

"Perfect," she said, giving me a quick hug before heading toward the door. "I'll let you get back to it. Thanks, Abby."

As she left, the weight of the catering job ahead of me settled back onto my shoulders. I didn't have much time to linger on thoughts of Christmas dinner. Right now, I had to focus on Ellie's baby shower, and my prep list was staring me down like a mountain I had to climb.

I turned my attention to the chicken, which I'd roasted earlier for the chicken salad and waffle skewers. I sliced and chopped it all then made two piles, one for the salad and one for the skewers. It was comforting in a way, but my mind kept wandering back to the murders.

This Trent person kept coming to mind. Did he have something to do with all this? What was his relationship to Katherine and Kelly? Or Charles? Were they still in contact? And was he even in Sugar Creek anymore?

The champagne had been sitting out in plain sight—anyone could have tampered with it. My mind kept circling back to that detail, too. It was a huge sticky problem and I couldn't see my way through it.

And what about Ryan? Guilt tugged at me again as I thought about how I'd snapped at him. He hadn't believed me about the car, and that had hurt. But he had so much on his plate—a murder investigation, now two, not to mention Katherine's drama. I needed to cut him some slack. He was doing his best, just like I was.

After I finished with the chicken tasks, I cleaned my hands and then moved on to prepping the puff pastry cups, pressing them into tiny tart pans with quick, precise motions. This was where I thrived—in the kitchen, making sure every detail was perfect. And yet, no matter how much I threw myself into the work, the questions still nagged at the back of my mind.

Was Brittney involved? It didn't make sense for her to kill Charles, especially if they were in a relationship. Unless... unless she was trying to kill Katherine and accidentally poisoned Charles instead. But even then, she would have known the champagne was meant for Charles.

I shook my head, frustrated. There were too many loose ends, too many possibilities. I didn't envy Ryan trying to piece it all together.

A little while later, as I wrapped the apple hand pies and popped them into the oven, I glanced at the clock. Time was running out. I needed to pack everything up, load the van, and head over to Ellie's before I risked being late. There was no room for mistakes today—not when this event was for one of my closest friends.

With a deep breath, I wiped my hands on a towel, grabbed my keys, and started loading the trays into the van. It was going to be tight, but if I hustled, I could make it work. And maybe, just maybe, I could push all the chaos of the last few days to the back of my mind long enough to pull off the perfect baby shower.

Chapter Twenty-Four

Despite my foray into amateur sleuthing with Cassie, I managed to get to Ellie's house earlier than strictly necessary to set up the catering for the party. I selfishly wanted to hang out with the mother-to-be a little bit before the rest of the group showed up, so I was glad I pulled it off. Ellie had found a lovely manager a few months back to take over the Sugar Creek Bakery for her, and I missed seeing her smiling face at my frequent stops there.

The temperature had dropped several degrees since I left Primrose House. I rubbed my hands together against the chill as I walked to the back of the van for supplies after parking at the curb, mentally checking my to-do list for the party. Just as I was about to open the back door, I felt it—a prickling sensation at the nape of my neck. A car passed by slowly, its headlights illuminating the front of the house.

My heart stuttered in my chest. I watched the car, my breath catching as it circled the block and passed again. This time, I caught a better look. It was a dark sedan, the same make and model as the one that had followed me yesterday. Was this a coincidence?

Ryan's words echoed in my mind, his dismissal of the stalker theory... but my instincts were screaming at me.

I shook my head, pushing the fear down. Maybe it really was nothing—Sugar Creek was a small town, and there were plenty of cars that looked like that. I couldn't go jumping at every shadow just because of Katherine's paranoia.

Steeling myself, I turned my attention back to the task at hand. No time for drama tonight. Ellie was counting on me to make this party perfect.

I grabbed a couple of catering bags from the back of my van and headed toward the house. Ellie was already waiting at the door, her glowing smile momentarily distracting me from my lingering unease.

"You're early!" she said, beaming as she waved me inside.

"I couldn't stay away," I replied with a grin, stepping into the warmth of her cozy home. "Besides, I wanted to spend a little time with you before the rest of the ladies showed up."

Ellie laughed as she rubbed her round belly. "I'm glad you did. Once they get here, I'm going to be swamped with belly rubs and unsolicited advice."

I set the bags down on the dining table, casting a glance around the room. Ellie had already decorated with twinkling Christmas lights and festive garlands, giving the house a cozy, magical feel. Soft holiday music played in the background, adding to the atmosphere.

"I love what you've done with the place," I said. "It's perfect for the baby shower."

Ellie smiled, watching me as I unpacked the trays of food. "Thanks. I can't believe this little guy is almost here. Time's flown by."

I chuckled. "Seems like just yesterday you were running the bakery, and now look at you—getting ready to be a mom."

Ellie sighed, a wistful look in her eyes. "Yeah, I miss the bakery sometimes. But I'm so ready for this new chapter. I can't wait to meet him."

As we talked, there was a knock at the door, and I smiled. "That'll be Cassie. She promised she'd come early to help me set up."

Ellie's face brightened. "Good! More hands to make light work."

I wiped my hands on a kitchen towel as Ellie went to open the door. Cassie breezed in, her cheeks flushed from the cold, and grinned when she saw me.

"Hey there! I brought reinforcements," she said, holding up a tray of cookies. "And yes, I made them myself. Don't look so surprised."

I laughed, grateful for her presence. "I wouldn't dream of it. I could definitely use the extra help. And the extra sugar."

Cassie set her tray down on the counter and took a quick look around. "Wow, everything looks amazing in here. You've really outdone yourself this time, Abby."

"Thanks, but we still have a lot to do before the guests get here," I replied. "Grab an apron, we've got work to do."

We finished laying out the food while Ellie hovered nearby, her eyes glowing with anticipation.

As we worked, Ellie leaned against the counter and asked, "What's Aunt Meg up to tonight?"

"She's got a house full of crazy right now, including a Broadway diva who's..." I hesitated and widened my eyes, glancing at Cassie, who grinned knowingly.

Ellie's eyes widened. "I heard about that whole thing with the Broadway star! What a tragedy. I can't imagine. She must be mourning her sister. I'm surprised she's still doing that show. If it were me, I'd be out of there in a heartbeat."

Cassie laughed. "Yeah, you'd think. But Katherine's more concerned with the show than anything else. If she's grieving, she's not showing it."

"Does this have alcohol in it?" Ellie asked as she unconsciously patted her large stomach, motioning to the bowl of eggnog I'd set out.

"Nope! I brought some that people can add to the side, but this should be safe for you," I reassured her.

Ellie's brow furrowed as she ladled herself a glass. "You know, my brother Bobby dated her for a while in high school?"

Cassie's eyebrows shot up. "Really? Katherine or Kelly?"

"Katherine, although we all called her Kitty back then. Guess she ditched the name when she moved away. Their thing didn't last long. Even back then, she had a way about her. Too good for us all, you know?"

I nodded, thinking back to Charles calling her 'Kitty' when we first arrived at the theater. "Yeah, I heard Charles call her Kitty, too. She didn't seem to like it much."

Before I could respond, the doorbell rang again, and Ellie's face brightened with excitement. "Party time!"

Cassie helped me set the final trays of food on the dining table as more guests arrived, leaving the conversation about Katherine hanging in the air.

The room hummed with lively conversation, and I felt a wave of pride at how everything had come together. Ellie's shower was a success, and seeing her surrounded by friends, laughing and glowing, made all the hard work worth it. Cassie nudged me with her elbow as she popped a mini quiche into her mouth. "Everything looks amazing, as usual. You've got a serious talent, Abby."

"Thanks," I said, though my mind was already drifting back to everything happening with Katherine and the theater. No matter how much I tried to stay focused on the party, the mystery kept tugging at the edges of my thoughts.

Just then, Cassie's cousin Melissa wandered over, carrying a glass of punch and grinning at us. "You guys look like you're deep in thought," she teased. "Hope you're not plotting anything too serious over baby shower appetizers."

Cassie gave her a quick smile. "You know us too well, Melissa. But actually, we were talking about the theater stuff. So you said you knew them in high school?"

Melissa's eyebrows shot up. "Yeah, right? Crazy stuff about her and Kelly...and now Charles. I heard about that." Her face turned down. "I was in drama with them all for a year in high school. Kitty had drama in her blood—couldn't get enough of the spotlight."

Cassie glanced at me, then asked, "Did you know her well?"

Melissa shrugged. "As well as anyone around here did, I guess. She was always a bit...distant. But Kelly was different. More approachable, down-to-earth. Honestly, Kelly wanted it all just as much as Katherine did—maybe even more, the theater, the spotlight. But Katherine had something about her, you know? That 'it' factor. Even back then, you could tell she was going to make it big."

I chewed on my lip, thinking. "What about Charles?"

Melissa let out a small laugh. "Oh yeah, Charles was always there in the theater group, too. Always trying to upstage everyone. He wasn't half as talented as he thought he was, but that didn't stop him from trying to make everything about him."

I nodded, filing the information away. "And what about the rest of the group? Was there anyone else who was close to them?"

For a moment, Melissa's eyes brightened as if something clicked. "Actually, there was this one kid—Trent Morrison. He was always hanging around, trying to break into their little group, but they never really accepted him. He was an outsider, no matter how hard he tried. It was sad, really."

I exchanged a glance with Cassie, and I could tell we were both thinking the same thing. "Do you think Trent would still hold a grudge about being left out after all these years?"

Melissa hesitated, her gaze flicking between the two of us. "I don't know. It's hard to say. People hold on to things longer than you think, sometimes." She took a sip of her punch, then added,

"But he's still around, you know. Lives in the same house he grew up in. Over on Willow Street, I think. Kinda keeps to himself these days."

Cassie and I shared a significant look. I had no doubt that tomorrow, we'd be paying Trent Morrison a visit.

"Anyway, that's about all I know. You going to your parents' place for Christmas?" she asked Cassie as she bit into a waffle and chicken skewer.

"Nah, going to Dallas with Ty. You going to be there?"

Melissa nodded. "Yep, taking the whole family over. Well, good to talk to you both. Keep me posted on what you find out, alright?"

Cassie grinned and nodded, then gave her a hug. We stood together a moment, processing what Melissa had said as we watched the party winding down. The guests were beginning to mingle less and gather their things more. After the gifts were opened and plenty of hugs were exchanged, Ellie's mother tapped a champagne glass to get everyone's attention. "Alright, y'all! Time for one last toast before we wrap this up. Fill your glasses— whether it's punch or the real deal—and come join us in the living room."

Everyone gathered, lifting their glasses in celebration, and the room buzzed with laughter and good cheer. I smiled at the warmth and love in the air, but my mind was already turning over the new information we'd just learned.

As the guests began to file out, I started to clean up the leftover trays of food, boxing up extras for Ellie and her husband. There was still more than enough to go around, and I hated the idea of it going to waste.

Cassie came over a few minutes later to help. "I've been thinking," she said, lowering her voice. "What if we took some of these leftovers to the police station? It'd be a good excuse to show up without looking suspicious, and I bet we'll catch Ryan or Ty there."

I raised an eyebrow. "Oh, so this is about food, huh?"

Cassie grinned. "I mean, food and information gathering can go hand in hand, right?"

I laughed, shaking my head. "Fine. But only if you promise not to drag me into another investigation tonight. I've got enough on my plate."

She held up her hands in mock surrender. "Promise."

Once we'd packed up the leftovers and said our goodbyes to Ellie, I felt a wave of satisfaction. The party had gone off without a hitch, and despite the weight of everything happening with Katherine and the theater, I'd managed to put it aside long enough to enjoy the evening.

But now, as we packed up my van with the extra trays, the weight of the mystery returned. Trent Morrison was on my mind, and so was the car that had passed earlier. Could they be connected? We would find out soon enough, I thought.

Cassie closed the back of the van and turned to me, her eyes gleaming. "Ready?"

"Ready," I replied, my mind already racing ahead to our next move.

CHAPTER TWENTY-FIVE

The night was downright cold as Cassie and I pulled up to the Sugar Creek Police Station a few minutes later, the December air crisp enough to bite at our cheeks. Our arms were loaded down with containers of leftovers from Ellie's baby shower, the warmth of the food only doing so much to keep the cold at bay. My breath puffed out in visible clouds as we hurried toward the entrance.

"I hope they're hungry," Cassie said, juggling a precarious stack of plastic containers filled with mini waffle skewers and divinity. Her breath was coming out in quick little bursts, more from excitement than from the cold.

"After the day they've had, I bet they could use a pick-me-up," I replied, cradling the dessert trays like they were my personal offering to the universe. No doubt the station had been buzzing with Charles' death, and I figured a little comfort food couldn't hurt.

We pushed through the glass doors and were immediately greeted by the warm air and soft glow of Christmas lights. Irene looked up from her desk, her glasses perched on the end of her nose as she thumbed through a stack of papers. She raised an eyebrow and smiled when she saw us.

"Well, if it isn't Santa's little helpers," she said with a tired smile. "What've you got there?"

"Just some leftovers from Ellie's baby shower," I replied, setting my load down on a nearby desk. "We thought you all could use a snack."

"Leftovers?" Irene's face lit up, and she stood, stretching her back with a wince. "Bless you both. We've been eating vending machine junk for I don't know how long."

Cassie got straight to work setting up the spread. "Where are Ryan and Ty?" she asked, trying to sound casual, but I could hear the underlying edge of curiosity in her voice. She was here for more than just spreading cheer.

Irene jerked her thumb toward the back. "In Ryan's office. They've been going over new leads for hours." Her expression tightened just slightly, as if the weight of the case was resting on all of their shoulders.

I exchanged a glance with Cassie. This might be our chance to glean some information, but we'd have to play it cool.

"Good timing, then. Sounds like they could use a break," I said, handing Irene a plate. "Help yourself, please."

Irene sighed and took a bite of the chicken salad. "You know, they've been at it nonstop since Charles died. I don't think Ryan's eaten a thing all day. I'll call him."

She picked up the phone and when she connected to Ryan, she told him Cassie and I were here.

I bit my lip, knowing the last few days had been hard on him. The frustration about being warned off the case and having my concerns about the stalker brushed aside loosened. I knew they were all under a tremendous amount of stress and could use a little understanding.

A moment later, Ryan and Ty emerged from Ryan's office, both looking rumpled and worn.

"Hey, you two," Ryan said, smiling when he saw me. He looked tired, but his smile still had that special effect on me. "What's this? You brought us dinner?"

"Leftovers from the baby shower," I replied, holding up the tray of cookies and divinity. "We figured you all could use a little holiday cheer."

Ty grabbed Cassie and pulled her in for a kiss, then grabbed a handful of food like he hadn't eaten in days. "You're the best."

Cassie laughed. "Abby's the one who made the food. You should thank her."

He turned his gaze to me and put his hands together in thanks before popping a date into his mouth and closing his eyes as he chewed.

The two of them looked like they'd been through the wringer. It wasn't just the murder of Charles—it was the whole town buzzing about what might be happening behind the scenes, about Katherine, the stalker, and, of course, Kelly's death still hanging over everything. Probably the publicity of the whole thing, too. I didn't envy them. Not one bit.

Irene piled her plate high and then gave us all a little wave. "I'm heading back to the paper mines. Have fun, y'all!"

We waved to her and smiled, then I watched as the men tucked into the food.

"So," I ventured, keeping my voice light, "any updates? Unless you don't want to share, that is." I tried to keep the hurt out of my voice, but it wasn't easy.

Ryan sighed, running a hand through his hair, making it stick up even more than it already was. "We canvassed the theater tonight, before, during, and after the show. Still no sign of a stalker or anyone suspicious. We talked to the whole crew again. Not many people liked Charles, but I didn't get the sense that anyone hated him enough to kill him. Whatever the truth is, we've decided that the stalker angle is out."

Cassie and I exchanged a glance. Should we tell them about

Trent? Part of me wanted to spill everything, but I had a feeling Cassie wasn't ready to share that particular piece of information just yet. Honestly, I wasn't either. I wanted to dig a little more before making a fool of myself. So I decided to share something else instead. "We talked to Brittney a few days ago…"

Ryan's expression darkened, and he fixed me with a hard stare. "Y'all didn't! I specifically asked you not to pry this time!"

He was madder than a hornet and I couldn't blame him, but I dropped his hand, nonetheless. "We weren't prying," I said, lifting my chin. "We were talking to a friend." Well, "friend" was stretching it a bit, but it wasn't a lie either.

Ty raised an eyebrow. "A *friend*, huh? So, should we just take her off the suspect list then?"

Cassie crossed her arms, clearly bristling at Ty's tone. "You might want to," she shot back. "We don't think Brittney's involved."

Ty leaned back, giving her a look. "Oh yeah, Nancy Drew? Why's that?"

Cassie's face turned sour and I could tell she had her tail up. I hoped she would take it easy on the men. They'd had enough hardship, I figured, even if I didn't like their attitude either. I stepped in before the conversation could get any more heated.

"We agree about the stalker from New York," I said, wanting to give them something, but not everything. "We were thinking it might be somebody from Sugar Creek, actually. Who's stalking Katherine."

Ryan frowned. "You mean like Brittney?"

I shrugged. "Not exactly. We were thinking, what if it's someone else we haven't thought of? Someone from their past?"

Cassie glanced at me and sighed, clearly frustrated to be sharing her treasured information. But she did it anyway. "My cousin said something tonight about a Trent Morrison who used to pal around with the group in high school. She said he still lives in town."

Ryan straightened, clearly intrigued. "I haven't heard anything about a Trent Morrison. What all did you hear?"

"That he was part of the group back in high school, but on the periphery. I guess Katherine and Charles never really accepted him into their group."

"And you think that might lead him to kill them? I don't know, that feels like a stretch."

"It's hard to say about old grudges. Who knows what the man might be thinking? And who knows how unhinged he is?"

Cassie nodded, picking up the thread. "Yeah, maybe he saw Katherine coming back to Sugar Creek as his chance to get close again. Maybe even close enough to act. What if he's out for the whole group? What if he deliberately killed Kelly and Charles and Katherine is going to be next?"

Ty let out a low whistle. "Well, that's one heck of a theory, but stranger things have happened."

Ryan's eyes narrowed, and he stood up straighter, clearly considering the possibility. "It's a long shot, but it's not impossible. I suppose if he's a local who's been around the theater in the past, that could explain why nobody noticed him."

I felt my heart race at the thought. We were close—closer than we had been all week. "So what now? How do we find him?"

Ryan exchanged a glance with Ty, who gave a slight nod. "*We* don't find anyone." He gestured at Ty and then at himself. "We, as in the Sugar Creek Sheriff's Office, will look into this Trent Morrison, see if he's been around, and if anyone's seen him near Katherine lately. I'll pull what I can from our system and check out any leads if they exist. But I want y'all to stay out of it. I can see your wheels turning, both of you. This isn't for you, am I clear?"

Cassie bristled beside me, and I felt my own frustration rising. He was brushing us off again. After everything we'd done, all the clues we'd uncovered, he still didn't take us seriously. It hurt more than I wanted to admit.

"Stay out of it?" Cassie echoed, her voice sharp. "Ryan, we're not meddling for the fun of it. This guy could be dangerous."

Ryan sighed, clearly exasperated but trying to stay calm. "I know you mean well, but this is police work. You've already done enough by bringing us this lead. Let us handle it from here."

I bit my tongue, fighting the urge to argue. Ryan's protectiveness was showing, and while I understood where he was coming from, it still stung to be sidelined. But I couldn't let this turn into a fight. Not now.

I took a deep breath, trying to keep my voice steady. "We just want to help, Ryan. We've been in the middle of this from the start, and I can't just sit back and pretend we're not part of it."

Ty, sensing the tension, stepped in, his voice gentler than usual. "Look, we appreciate everything you've done, but we don't want you two in harm's way. This guy—if he's the one we're after—he's already hurt people. We can't risk you getting caught up in that."

The logic made sense, but it didn't soothe the burn of being left out. Cassie and I exchanged a look, both of us silently agreeing to let the conversation drop for now. There was no winning this argument tonight.

"Well," I said finally, my voice tight, "I guess we'll leave it to you then."

Ty grabbed another skewer, giving me a grateful nod. "Thanks again for the food, Abby. It's keeping us going."

I packed up the remaining containers, the tension in my shoulders refusing to ease. "We'll leave these here for you later. You'll need something to keep you going through the night."

Ryan's eyes softened as he reached for my hand, his touch warm but exhausted. "I mean it. Thank you for this," he said quietly, squeezing my hand gently. "I know it's been a rough few days."

I gave him a small smile, though my heart still felt heavy. "Just... make sure you actually eat something, okay?"

He nodded, but his eyes lingered on mine a little longer, as if he wanted to say something else. I pulled away before he could, the sting of being pushed aside still too raw.

Cassie was already halfway to the door, eager to escape the serious atmosphere of the station. "Come on, Abby. We've got theories to work through."

I laughed, following her toward the door. "You mean we're going to sit on my couch, eat leftover sweets, and rehash this until midnight?"

"That's exactly what I mean." Cassie winked, and with a final wave to Ty and Ryan, we stepped out into the chilly night.

The cold air hit me the moment we exited the station, a reminder of how far into winter we were. The stars peeked through the clouds, and the streets were quiet, lit only by the soft glow of holiday lights strung across shop windows.

As we walked to the van, Cassie nudged me. "You know, we're getting closer. I can feel it."

I nodded, breathing in the cold air, letting the weight of the day fall off my shoulders. "Yeah, I think you're right. But something tells me this is going to get a lot messier before it gets clearer."

Cassie grinned. "Good thing we're great at cleaning up messes."

I unlocked the van, and we climbed in, cranking up the heat as the engine roared to life. I glanced back at the station through the rearview mirror, the twinkling Christmas lights casting everything in a warm glow.

Messy or not, I knew we were inching closer to the truth. And something told me, in the pit of my stomach, that when it all came to light, it was going to hit a lot harder than any of us expected.

CHAPTER TWENTY-SIX

Christmas Eve dawned with the kind of peaceful quiet that felt rare in Sugar Creek these days. After everything that had happened—the murders, the chaos at the theater, and now the wrap party to prep for—I was ready for a distraction. And what better way to spend Christmas Eve than baking and making sure the town had plenty of food to celebrate?

I made my way over to Primrose House as early as I dared, hoping I wouldn't wake anyone. The air was cold, the sky lit up with the faintest hints of light peeking over the horizon. Snow was actually in the forecast, surprising every one of us, but whether it would come in time for Christmas or not was still anyone's guess. I could only hope it wouldn't mess with the party plans.

Saturday morning was normally quiet on Main Street, but this morning as I passed the small shops and restaurants I noticed many more lights on, business owners hoping to take advantage of the last-minute shoppers, no doubt.

A few lights were on in the windows of Primrose House too, as I parked in the lot. Pushing open the front door, I immediately felt that warm, cozy feeling that only Aunt Meg's house could give me. I breathed it in deeply, trying to shake off the slight chill that still clung to me from the early morning. To my surprise, the soft clinking of dishes and the low hum of Christmas music told me I wasn't the only one awake.

Aunt Meg was already in the kitchen, humming quietly as she stood by the stove, stirring a pot of what smelled like spiced cider. She looked up with a bright smile when she saw me.

"Well, good morning, Abby! I didn't expect you this early, but I'm glad you're here." She gave the pot one last stir before wiping her hands on her apron and turning toward me. "You ready for all the madness you got going on today?"

I set my bags down on the counter, filled with ingredients for the final round of cooking I had to do before the wrap party. "Yeah, but I wanted to get a head start. I've still got appetizers and a few desserts to finish before this evening. Plus, you know, it's Christmas Eve, so..." I trailed off with a smile. "Who knows what else is in store for the day?"

Aunt Meg chuckled softly. "Always busy, that's my girl. I've got a few things planned for our guests today, too. We're going to do a special Christmas Eve tea in the parlor. I wanted to do something memorable for the Nagasaki family before they leave this afternoon. I've got the house decorated, and I'm making a few more treats before the festivities kick off."

I smiled, knowing how much Aunt Meg loved making her guests feel special. "That sounds lovely. I'm sure they'll love it. I'll have to stop in if I can manage to steal a few minutes."

"You'll be lucky if you even have time to breathe today," Aunt Meg teased, but her smile faltered for a moment. "How are you holding up with everything going on? I know the murders have been weighing on everyone."

I paused, glancing out the kitchen window where the trees swayed gently in the crisp morning breeze. "It's been... a lot. I'm just hoping tonight's wrap party goes smoothly, you know? Everyone's on edge with what's happened. It'll be nice to close this chapter. I know Ryan and Ty are working hard on getting it all sorted." And on keeping Cassie and I out of things, I thought grumpily.

Aunt Meg nodded in understanding, her eyes softening. "I think you're right, dear. Everyone could use a little bit of peace right now. Especially Katherine, I'm sure."

Before I could respond, a sudden, piercing scream cut through the quiet morning air, sending a jolt of shock straight through me.

My heart leaped into my throat as I locked eyes with Aunt Meg, her expression mirroring my own alarm. Without thinking, I darted toward the front of the house, my legs moving faster than my mind could catch up. The sound had come from the porch.

I threw open the front door and stumbled onto the porch, my breath catching in my chest. A couple of guests were already gathered around, their faces pale and drawn as they stood in a tight huddle. At their feet, sprawled across the porch like some horrible offering, was a dead raccoon.

And standing over it, her entire body trembling, was Katherine.

I pushed my way through the small crowd, my stomach twisting as I saw the lifeless animal up close. Its fur was matted, and the way it had been laid out was too deliberate to be an accident. And it hadn't been on the porch only a little while before when I'd arrived, which was very strange.

My eyes shifted from the raccoon to Katherine, who stood frozen, a crumpled piece of red paper clutched in her hand. Her face was pale as she stared down at the raccoon, her lips pressed tightly together in a thin line.

"Katherine?" I asked gently, moving closer. "What happened?"

She met my gaze, her eyes wide with a mix of horror and anger. Her hand shook as she handed me the red piece of paper. "For the Diva," she whispered, her voice trembling. "It's from... *him*. The stalker. It must be."

I took the note from her, my stomach sinking as I read the words. *For the Diva*. The words were scrawled hastily across the red paper, the ink smudged in places. My mind raced as I tried to process it. Was this a message? A warning?

"I... I don't know what this is," I said, frowning as I looked up at Katherine. "You think it's from the stalker?"

Katherine's face contorted into a grimace of frustration. "Of course it is! Who else would send me something like this?" She threw her hands up, pacing the porch as the other guests looked on, clearly unsure of what to say. "This town! It never changes!"

Aunt Meg appeared behind me, her face drawn with concern as she surveyed the scene. "Oh, my. A dead raccoon? In broad daylight? Y'all sure it wasn't meant as a gift?"

Katherine's face registered shock, crossing her arms tightly over her chest. "Who in their right mind would think this was a gift? This is a threat! I've had enough of these sick games."

Aunt Meg's voice was calm, though I could see the worry in her eyes. "Well, dear, people around here are strange, I agree. But it's not entirely clear what the intent was..."

Katherine growled in frustration, cutting Aunt Meg off and casting one last look at the raccoon before stomping back into the house, muttering under her breath. The small crowd dispersed slowly, with murmurs of unease following them.

I stayed on the porch, the cold air nipping at my cheeks as I tried to make sense of it all. A dead raccoon and a cryptic note. Yet another piece of a weird puzzle that didn't seem to fit. I called Ryan and told him briefly about what had transpired and then headed inside to wait for him and warm up.

Ten minutes later, Ryan arrived, his face set in that professional calm I'd come to rely on. He stepped onto the porch and surveyed the scene, his eyes immediately landing on the raccoon.

"Well, this is new," he muttered, pulling on a pair of gloves as he crouched down by the animal. "Who found it?"

"Katherine," I said, stepping back slightly to give him room. "She came out here and found it with this note." I held up the red paper for him to see.

Ryan frowned as he read it, his eyes narrowing. "For the Diva...?"

"She thinks it's from her stalker," I explained, lowering my voice as I watched Ryan examine the animal.

Ryan's expression was grim as he stood up, his gaze shifting from the raccoon to the porch. "We'll take this seriously. There's no telling if it's connected to everything else that's happened, but it's definitely not something we're going to ignore."

I wanted to ask him about Trent Morrison, whether he thought this could be related or whether he'd had time to look into the man yet. But I held my tongue, not ready to get into all that with him again.

Aunt Meg nodded beside me. "It's unsettling, that's for sure."

Ryan sighed, glancing over at me. "I'll dispose of the raccoon. We'll look into it, but for now, try to keep an eye on Katherine. She's shaken up, I'm sure."

I nodded, my stomach still unsettled by the whole thing. After Ryan left, the porch slowly cleared, and I found myself standing alone, shivering slightly as the cold air swirled around me. The sky had darkened even more, the promise of snow heavy in the clouds.

I stood there for a moment longer, staring at the empty spot where the raccoon had been before heading back inside to the warmth of the kitchen. I still had a party to prepare for, and as much as the dead raccoon rattled me, I couldn't let it throw me off my game. There was too much to do.

With a deep breath, I picked up my knife and returned to chopping, though my mind couldn't quite shake the lingering unease that clung to the morning.

Time passed in a blur of chopping, stirring, and frantic organization as I worked on the food for the wrap party. The kitchen was a whirlwind of activity, with counters cluttered with trays, bowls, and cooling racks. Christmas Eve and the final show—it was going to be one of the busiest days of the year. Luckily, I had plenty of energy between the time pressure and the adrenaline from the raccoon incident.

I wiped my hands on my apron, pausing for a moment to glance over the spread I'd already assembled on the large kitchen island. Everything had to be perfect, not just for the party but because it was the theater's wrap party—a big deal, even with the cloud of tragedy hanging over the event. I wanted the food to reflect the flair and drama of the theater itself, so I'd gone for a full-on performance with the menu.

The star of the buffet were my *Stage Left Sliders*, tiny brioche buns filled with juicy roast beef, caramelized onions, and horse-radish cream. I'd skewered them with little toothpicks that had tiny red flags mimicking the velvet curtains of the theater. It was all in the details.

On the opposite side of the island, I'd started to assemble my *Bravo Brie Bites*—puff pastry cups filled with melted brie and cranberry sauce—when my mind began to wander again. The image of the dead raccoon on the porch, Katherine's trembling hands, and the note scrawled with *For the Diva* flashed through my mind.

A shiver ran down my spine as I thought about it. I had a pretty good idea of who was behind the whole thing now, but doubt kept creeping in. Trent Morrison. He was an outsider, one who had wanted to be part of the group but had been shut out. It made sense in a twisted way. Trent could have carried that resentment for years, and now, with the Kirby sisters back in town, maybe he saw his chance to strike.

But then again, how deep could that grudge really go? Sure, Trent had been ignored and rejected in high school, but was that enough for him to become a stalker? To send threatening notes and leave a dead animal on a doorstep? To kill people, even?

I brushed off a stray crumb from one of the trays, my thoughts circling around the same uneasy questions. Had Ryan talked to Trent yet? Did he even know where to find him? He hadn't mentioned anything when he'd come about the raccoon, but that didn't mean he wasn't looking into it. I trusted Ryan, but it was hard not to let my mind race when we were running out of time to figure out who was behind all this.

I glanced at the clock—almost noon. The show would be starting before too long, and I still had plenty to do before the party. But no matter how busy I kept myself, the uneasy feeling gnawed at the back of my mind.

I turned back to the table and started arranging the *Curtain Call Cookies*—buttery sugar cookies shaped like little theater masks and stars, with brightly colored icing and edible glitter. The cookies sparkled under the kitchen lights, but even the cheerful sight didn't ease the knot of tension in my stomach.

The trays of food sat gleaming under the soft kitchen lights, and I let out a breath, willing myself to refocus. There was still so much to do, and the party was just hours away. But even with the kitchen buzzing around me, I couldn't shake the feeling that something was going to happen. Something bigger.

I wiped my hands on a dish towel, glancing out the window at the fading winter light. Time was slipping away, and the weight of everything was pressing down on me. The wrap party, the strange notes, Trent, Katherine's nervousness—it all swirled in my mind like a puzzle I couldn't quite solve.

Just as I grabbed another tray of the brie bites to finish assembling, the door swung open behind me, and I turned to find Cassie slipping in, her expression determined as always.

"Hey, got a minute?"

I sighed and put the brie down.

CHAPTER TWENTY-SEVEN

I wiped my hands on a towel, trying to keep my voice steady. "I'm up to my elbows in catering. What's going on?"

She pulled out a chair and sat at the kitchen table, her eyes full of purpose. "I found out where Trent lives."

I froze for a second, the knot in my stomach tightening. "And?"

"And I think we should go talk to him," she said, leaning forward. "Today."

My heart skipped a beat. The last thing I wanted to do was confront Trent, especially with everything that had happened. "Cassie, I don't know. Ryan and Ty already told us specifically not to get involved with him, and I've got so much to do before the party."

Cassie raised an eyebrow, watching me closely. "There's something you're not telling me, Abby. What is it?"

I sighed, knowing she'd see right through any attempt to brush her off. "Okay, something weird happened this morning. A dead raccoon showed up on the porch of Primrose House. And there was a note with it."

Cassie's eyes widened. "A dead raccoon? What did the note say?"

"It said, 'For the Diva.'" I grimaced at the memory. "Aunt Meg and I weren't sure if it was a threat or some kind of twisted gift. Ryan thought it was definitely a threat."

Cassie's jaw dropped. "Why didn't you tell me about this sooner? A dead animal and a note? That's seriously creepy!"

I shrugged helplessly. "I didn't want to make a big deal out of it. But now, I'm starting to wonder if it was Trent. I mean, who else would do something like that?"

Cassie's eyes lit up with determination. "That settles it. We have to go talk to him."

I shook my head, anxiety bubbling in my chest. "Cassie, what if he's dangerous? We should just let Ryan handle it."

But Cassie leaned forward, her voice firm. "Abby, this guy left a dead raccoon on your porch! He's escalating. If we wait for Ryan, we might miss our chance to find out what's really going on. We're not accusing him of anything—we're just going to ask a few questions."

I bit my lip, torn between my fear and the logic of what Cassie was saying. She was right—we couldn't just sit around and hope someone else would figure it out. "Fine," I said, throwing my hands up in defeat. "But we're keeping it short. I have a lot to do, and I'm already running behind."

Cassie grinned, her excitement bubbling over. "Deal. Quick and easy."

The drive to Trent's house was tense, neither of us saying much as Cassie navigated through the quiet streets. My thoughts kept drifting back to the dead raccoon, the note, and now this confrontation. What if Trent really was behind everything?

Cassie pulled up to Trent's house, a worn-down place on the outskirts of town, and my stomach twisted with nerves. But what made me freeze in place was the sight of the car parked in front of the house.

"That's the car," I whispered, my voice barely audible. "That's the one that's been following me."

Cassie sucked in a breath. "Are you sure?"

I nodded, my heart hammering in my chest. "It's definitely the same car."

Cassie frowned, glancing between the car and the house. "Well, that confirms it. We *have* to talk to him now."

Panic surged through me, and I grabbed her arm. "Cassie, wait. We should go get Ryan. We can't just walk up there and confront him. What if he's dangerous?"

Cassie met my gaze, her eyes sharp with determination. "We're not confronting him. We're asking questions. We have a right to do that. Look, if we go get Ryan, we might lose our chance to catch Trent off guard. He's not expecting us, and if we're careful, we can keep it from escalating."

I shook my head, fear knotting my insides. "I don't know..."

Cassie gave me a serious look. "We can't let this go. Not now. If he's involved in all of this, we need to figure out how. You know I'm right."

I stared at her, my heart pounding. She *was* probably right, but that didn't make it any less terrifying. "Okay," I finally agreed, my voice shaky. "But we're in and out. No risks."

Cassie smiled grimly. "Promise."

We stepped out of the truck, the cold air biting at my skin as we walked toward Trent's house. My legs felt like lead as we approached the porch, my mind racing with every worst-case scenario. But Cassie, ever bold, knocked on the door before I could say a word.

For a long, agonizing moment, nothing happened.

Then, the door creaked open just a crack, and a man's face appeared in the narrow gap. His appearance startled me—he was wearing stage makeup, with dark eyeliner and pale lipstick, his face almost ghostly under the soft light from inside.

"Can I help you?" he asked, his voice polite but distant.

Cassie spoke first, her voice strong. "Hey, Trent. We're friends of Katherine's, and we wanted to ask you a few questions."

"I'm sorry," Trent said, his voice flat. "I can't talk right now. I'm preparing for a role."

I exchanged a confused glance with Cassie. "A role? What kind of role?"

Trent's eyes flickered, and he smiled—though it didn't reach his eyes. "Oh, not a play at the theater. Something... bigger."

My heart thudded in my chest. His words were strange, cryptic, and unsettling.

Cassie, always quick on her feet, forced a smile. "Right. Well, we don't want to interrupt. We'll leave you to it."

Trent's head tilted slightly, his makeup giving him an eerie, doll-like appearance. "Thank you. Have a good day."

The door clicked shut, and Cassie and I stood there for a moment, both of us tense and rattled.

"That was weird," I muttered, still processing what had just happened.

Cassie nodded, her face pale. "Yeah. Really weird. And I don't like it."

We hurried back to the truck, my heart racing the entire time. Trent's made-up face and cryptic comments clung to me, making it hard to shake the growing sense of unease.

As Cassie started the engine, the silence between us felt thick, both of us processing what had just happened. I kept glancing over my shoulder, expecting that same car—the one that had been following me—to appear out of nowhere. But the road behind us was still empty.

Cassie finally broke the tension. "He's got to be the stalker, Abby. Not only was he super weird, that was the same car that's been following you. It all adds up."

I nodded slowly, staring out the window. "Yeah, I'm sure of it now. And the makeup, the way he talked about 'a bigger role'... It's like he's not even living in reality."

"He's unhinged," Cassie muttered, gripping the steering wheel a little tighter. "What if he's planning something for tonight? It's the last show, the wrap party—everything's coming to a head."

I swallowed, the weight of her words settling in my chest. "Do you think he's going to try to kill Katherine? That's what this has been about all along, right?"

Cassie shot me a sidelong glance. "I don't know, but we can't just wait around to find out. I mean, he's wearing makeup like he's playing some twisted part. I don't like it."

A chill ran down my spine at the thought. "Final night of the show... it feels like he's building up to something. We have to stop him before he does anything worse."

Cassie nodded. "We need to call Ryan and Ty. Tell them everything—about Trent, the car, the whole thing."

I let out a long sigh, my stomach twisting into knots. "Yeah, you're right. But you know they're going to be mad when they find out we went to Trent's house. We broke the rules."

Cassie shrugged. "Better they be mad than someone else getting hurt. I'll call Ty and explain. It's important they know what we saw. We might be the only reason they catch Trent before it's too late."

I nodded, feeling the pressure weighing heavily on me. "You're right. I just... I really have to get back to work. There's still so much to do before the wrap party tonight."

Cassie pulled up in front of Primrose House and cut the engine, turning to me with a serious look in her eyes. "Go do what you need to do. I'll handle the call."

I smiled, grateful for her level-headedness in the midst of all the chaos. "Thanks. Just... make sure they understand how serious this is."

Cassie gave me a reassuring nod. "I'll get the message across. Go make that party happen, and we'll take care of this."

I stepped out of the truck and watched as Cassie pulled out her phone, already dialing Ty's number as she leaned against the driver's side door. My stomach churned with nerves, but I knew I had to trust her.

With a deep breath, I turned and headed back inside, ready to focus on the party. But no matter how hard I tried, the image of Trent's painted face and his strange, cryptic words wouldn't leave me. Something told me we were running out of time.

CHAPTER TWENTY-EIGHT

By the time I pulled up in front of the theater a couple of hours later, the clouds had darkened even more, though precipitation hadn't started yet. It had been a hectic few hours of prep work and constant phone checking, but despite Cassie's promise to get in touch with Ryan and Ty and to update me, I hadn't heard a peep.

I could hear the faint murmur of the show's dialogue and the sound of scattered applause from inside the theater as I stepped into the lobby. I figured that meant that Katherine was safe for now, since she was more than likely in the middle of the final performance. At least the show was going smoothly, for now. But it was time for my big catering role and I hoped against hope that things would work out.

My spirits rose as I found two people dressed in the all-black uniform of the catering professional waiting for me in the lobby. I recognized Jake from a few other events I'd catered, his cheerful grin as wide as ever. He would be the bartender for the evening. A young woman stood beside him, her quiet demeanor in sharp contrast.

"Hey there," Jake greeted me, giving me a nod. "You made it just in time."

"Barely," I said with a tired smile, adjusting the trays in my hands. "Thanks for meeting me here. We've got a lot to set up before the show lets out."

Leslie stepped forward, her voice soft but polite. "I'm Leslie. Jake's told me a lot about your work. It's nice to meet you."

"Nice to meet you, too," I said, shifting the trays to one side and extending a hand. "Thanks for helping out tonight. I think we're going to need all hands on deck."

I led them through the backstage corridors, the sound of the show still faintly audible from the stage as we made our way to the prop room. This was where the real work would happen—the wrap party wasn't just about the food, it was about making sure the cast and crew had something to celebrate after the emotional rollercoaster of the last few days. Even with all the tragedy, they deserved a proper sendoff.

The prop room was dimly lit, cluttered with pieces from past productions and mismatched furniture that we'd have to work around. I gestured to the far side of the room where we'd set up the buffet. "We'll start over here. I'll show you how I want everything arranged."

Jake whistled, taking in the space. "Not exactly glamorous, huh?"

I smiled despite myself. "It's a theater prop room. Glamour isn't really their style."

Leslie laughed lightly and nodded as I continued, "Okay, I've got trays of sliders, brie bites, cheese platters, fruit skewers, and a dessert spread that we'll set up over here." I motioned to the long table by the wall. "It's all buffet, no service. So that at least should lighten the load. Let's get everything unpacked and laid out. We'll want to be ready the minute the curtain drops."

They both nodded, and we quickly got to work. We all headed out to the van and started bringing everything inside. It only took a few trips between the three of us and I felt some of the pressure ease when everything at least was in the room.

Despite the dim lighting and the cluttered space, I felt a strange sense of control returning as we began setting up the buffet. For a moment, the familiar routine of catering washed over me, pushing the unease from earlier to the back of my mind.

But the quiet tension in the air, the absence of Ryan or any news, lingered like a dark cloud. Everything felt off despite my best attempts at control.

I glanced at Jake. "Alright, let's get you set up," I told him as we started to work the room. "The bar will be over here by the back wall. We'll keep it simple—wine, beer, a few basic mixed drinks. Plus eggnog that I've got. It's alcohol free, so you'll be in charge of adding alcohol and making sure nobody underage gets any. Just make sure to keep everything flowing, but not too fast. The last thing we need is people getting sloppy."

Jake nodded, his easygoing grin widening. "Got it, boss. Slow and steady."

I walked over to the small table set up near the wall and pointed out where I wanted the glasses and drinks arranged. He quickly got to work, his hands moving confidently as he started setting up the bottles and organizing the glasses into neat rows.

Leslie was already unpacking trays of sliders and brie bites, quietly but efficiently placing them on the buffet table. She looked up when I joined her. "Anything special you want with the desserts?"

"Yeah," I said, pointing to the far end of the table. "Let's keep the desserts over here, away from the savory items. Fruit skewers, cookies, and éclairs. Make sure the trays stay neat, even after people start digging in. Presentation is key. Oh, I have signage for everything, too." I rummaged in my bag and handed her some notecards I'd printed up with food labels and little stands to secure them with.

Leslie nodded and adjusted a platter of sliders before putting the cards in front of each type of food.

"Alright, we've got this," I said, half to them and half to myself, as I rubbed my hands together and glanced toward the door. The clock was ticking.

With a quick nod from both of them, we moved as a team to get everything situated. Then I went back out to the van to give it one last look and make sure we hadn't forgotten anything. I had a backup portable heater of appetizers there, but the case was too big to transport, so I left it in the van. I would come out and get backups if we needed them. The cold air outside contrasted to the warmth of the theater and made my cheeks flush and I scanned the parking lot, worried about Trent and Ryan and what might be happening without my knowledge. My nerves buzzed with the familiar tension that always accompanied a big event, but there was something more tonight—a sense of urgency, of something brewing just out of sight.

By the time I returned to the room, the setup was nearly complete. The buffet gleamed under the soft lights of the prop room, and Jake had the bar ready to go, his bottles lined up in perfect order.

I rubbed my hands together again, trying to shake the cold dread settling in my chest as I felt the clock counting down to the final curtain call. "Just keep an eye on the food," I reminded them. "Make sure it's replenished, but don't let anything sit out too long. And... keep an eye on the guests. I'm guessing this crowd might get a little rowdy after the final curtain call."

Jake chuckled, giving me a mock salute. "We've got your back."

Leslie smiled too, though there was a hint of nervousness in her eyes. "We're all set."

My gaze kept drifting to the door, waiting for any sign of Ryan, or some sign of something amiss. If Trent was going to do anything more, I was very confident that it would be during the final curtain call or the wrap party.

Jake must've noticed my preoccupation, because he cleared his throat. "Hey, Abby, you good?"

I forced another smile, but it felt brittle. "Yeah. Just a little anxious, I guess."

Leslie gave me a sympathetic look. "Big parties like this can be stressful. Especially when you're in charge of all the food. But don't worry—like Jake said, we've got your back."

"Thanks," I said, appreciating the reassurance, even though they had no idea what was really on my mind. "I just want everything to go smoothly."

As the two of them busied themselves with final touches, I stood back and let out a slow breath, running through every possible scenario in my mind. What if Trent showed up with something worse than a dead raccoon? What if Ryan couldn't stop him in time?

My thoughts were interrupted by the buzz of voices in the hall. The theater was starting to fill with the distant hum of conversation, the audience members trickling out of the final performance. The wrap party was moments away from starting, and all I could do was hope that the worst was behind us.

But the sinking feeling in my stomach told me otherwise.

CHAPTER TWENTY-NINE

I barely had time to brace myself before the door swung open a few minutes later, and the cast and crew started pouring in, still riding the high of the final performance. Laughter and chatter filled the air, mixing with the faint hum of Christmas music filtering in from the lobby. The low thrum of excitement buzzed through the room, and for a brief moment, it almost felt normal—like any other party I had catered. But the weight in my chest didn't lift.

Jake was already behind the bar, pouring drinks and handing them out with practiced ease. "Alright, folks! Drinks are ready. Let's celebrate!" His cheerful voice rang out, drawing people toward the bar like moths to a flame. I glanced over at the buffet table, where Leslie was making last-minute adjustments to the trays, her face calm and focused.

I didn't have time to think about Trent or Katherine as the guests streamed in. Actors, stagehands, and crew members surrounded the food table, eagerly grabbing at the trays of sliders and brie bites. I quickly moved to restock the platters as soon as they started to empty, my hands moving on autopilot as I tried to keep up with the demand.

"Hey caterer, these sliders are amazing!" one of the actors called out as he grabbed a second plate. "I don't know how you do it."

I flashed a quick smile. "Thanks! Glad you like them."

The compliments flowed, and I nodded and smiled where appropriate, but my mind was miles away. Where was Katherine? In all the chaos, I hadn't even seen a glimpse of her. Was she staying away from the party on purpose, or was something sinister happening beyond these happy walls? Was Trent still out there, somewhere in the dark, waiting to create chaos? *Already* creating chaos? The thought sent a shiver down my spine, but I couldn't afford to let it show. Not now.

Leslie stepped up beside me, carrying an empty tray back to the counter. "This crowd's hungrier than I expected," she said, flashing me a tired smile. "We're going to need more of those fruit skewers."

"On it," I said, reaching for the backup tray and swapping it out with the empty one.

More people filtered into the room, filling the air with laughter, excited chatter, and the occasional outburst of theatrical energy. The sound of clinking glasses and celebratory toasts echoed off the walls, adding to the festive atmosphere.

I caught Jake's eye across the room, and he gave me a quick thumbs-up, signaling that the bar was under control. At least that was one thing I didn't have to worry about.

Someone turned on a sound system and blasted the space with Christmas music. It reminded me of a scene from Breakfast at Tiffany's, minus the cigarette smoke, and it was all I could do to keep my balance as I weaved around the people drinking, dancing, talking way too loudly, and clowning around. The party was in full swing now, and I should have felt some relief that things were going smoothly. But instead, the pressure in my chest only grew. My eyes kept darting to the door, waiting for something—

anything—that would tell me Ryan was okay, that Trent had been dealt with, that Katherine wasn't in danger.

After about an hour, Leslie told me that the sliders were running out, so I decided to get the rest of the food from the van. I grabbed my keys and made my way toward the door. But as soon as I stepped out into the hallway, I knew something was going on. I booked it to the lobby, but stopped in my tracks when I saw what was happening.

Ryan was standing by the far corner with Ty by his side, and on the floor sat Trent—handcuffed, sobbing, and dressed in full costume.

But not just any costume.

He was dressed as Katherine.

The sight of him, with stage makeup smeared across his tear-streaked face and wearing a wig that was an eerie replica of Katherine's hair, sent a chill down my spine. My heart pounded in my chest, and I glanced between Ryan and Ty and Trent, unsure if I should be relieved or horrified by the scene in front of me.

"I didn't mean to hurt anyone," Trent sobbed, his voice trembling. "I was just playing a role. I was just doing what she told me."

Ryan's jaw tightened, but he kept his voice calm as he looked at Trent. "What role, Trent?"

Trent sniffled, blinking back more tears as he tried to explain. "Katherine... she told me to follow the caterer. She said she was nosy, always poking around and dating the sheriff. She said she would be the best person to spread the stalker story. I was playing the stalker role."

I felt the blood drain from my face as his words sank in. Follow the caterer... me. I'd been played.

But then his other words caught my attention, and I took a step back. *Katherine... I was just doing what she told me.*

Understanding dawned on me so suddenly, I felt like I needed to sit down.

Katherine had manipulated us all into thinking a stalker was after her. But why?

To get the focus off of herself, that's why. It came to me in a flash. The difficult relationship between the sisters, the frosty feelings between her and Charles. Could she have killed them?

Either way, I realized that I had been used as a pawn in Katherine's sick game of attention. My throat tightened, and shame rose in my chest, but I fought to keep my emotions in check.

Ryan shot me a quick glance, concern flashing in his eyes. I turned away, my cheeks burning with embarrassment. My busybody ways—snooping around and sticking my nose where it didn't belong—had been manipulated to fuel Katherine's lies.

But then, as Trent's sobbing continued, something else shifted in me. I thought back to the dead raccoon, the note, the stalking, and the unease I'd felt for days. If Trent hadn't been following me, if Katherine hadn't set me up as part of her charade, we might not have uncovered the truth at all.

I straightened my shoulders, squaring them against the shame trying to settle inside me. Yes, I had been used, but my actions had also led to this moment—this revelation. Katherine's plan had backfired.

Ryan turned his focus back to Trent, tightening his grip on the cuffs. "Why, Trent? Why'd you agree to it?"

Trent's tears slowed, and he looked up, eyes wide with a kind of dazed innocence that didn't quite fit the situation. "She needed me. Katherine... she said I could help her. That I could be part of the story." He swallowed hard, his voice barely a whisper. "I just wanted to play the role. I didn't mean anyone any harm. I didn't want to cause any trouble."

I watched him, pity mixing with the horror in my chest. It was clear that Trent had been twisted by Katherine's manipulation as well, pulled into a fantasy that had gone far beyond what he could control. But it didn't excuse what he'd done—the terror he'd caused, the part he had played in the chaos.

Ryan caught my eye again, his expression softening as he spoke. "Abby, you okay?"

I took a deep breath, still processing everything. "Yeah," I said quietly, though my heart was still pounding. "I'm okay. It's... it's just a lot."

Ryan gestured for Trent to stand and then motioned to Ty, who took Trent by the arm. Trent's sobs were quieter now, but his rambling about roles and scripts hadn't stopped.

"Take him down to the station. I'll be there soon, with any luck. And send a few more officers, too," Ryan told him. Ty gave me a grim nod before leading Trent toward the patrol car, leaving Ryan and me standing alone in the cool night.

Ryan turned to me, his voice low and serious. "Have you seen Katherine anywhere?"

I shook my head, the knot of tension tightening in my stomach. "No. Not all night. But I've been with the party the whole time. You think she's here?"

"She's supposed to be," he muttered, scanning the lobby as if she might appear from the shadows. "We need to find her."

The weight of his words settled over me like a heavy cloak. This wasn't just about stopping Trent anymore. Katherine was still out there, and after everything that had happened, she was very likely dangerous.

The task I'd come outside for was forgotten. Without another word, I fell in step beside Ryan, the two of us heading back toward the theater, our focus now entirely on finding Katherine before it was too late.

CHAPTER THIRTY

The theater felt impossibly quiet after the final show as Ryan and I stepped inside. The distant strains of laughter and conversation from the wrap party echoed faintly through the space, and I briefly felt a pang of guilt for leaving Jake and Leslie on their own. But beyond those comforting sounds, the rest of the building seemed shrouded in an eerie silence. Ryan and I moved together down the dimly lit corridor, our footsteps hushed on the worn floorboards.

"Katherine has to be here somewhere," Ryan muttered under his breath, his eyes scanning every shadowed corner. "She performed in the play. I saw her on stage earlier."

I nodded, though the tension in my chest made it hard to focus. After everything we had learned from Trent, it was clear that Katherine wasn't just hiding—she was running, and that thought chilled me to the bone. She wasn't someone who panicked easily, but now? Now she was desperate.

Ryan slowed to a stop, glancing back at me, concern etched on his face. "Abby, I don't think you should come with me for this. It's police business. I don't want you getting hurt."

I met his gaze, my heart pounding in my chest. "I can't just go back to the party and pretend everything is fine, Ryan. I'm safer with you than if I'm alone. Katherine's still out there, and who knows what she's planning?"

He hesitated, his jaw tightening. "It could get dangerous. You don't need to be in the middle of this."

"I'm already in the middle of it," I said firmly, stepping closer. "She's been manipulating us for days. You think she's just going to stop now? You heard Trent. They specifically targeted me. No, I'm staying right next to you."

Ryan studied me for a moment, his eyes searching mine. I could see the conflict in his expression—the protective instinct warring with the reality of the situation. Finally, he let out a sharp breath and gave a reluctant nod.

"Alright. But stay behind me, and if anything feels off, you get out of here. Promise me."

"I promise," I said, though my heart was still pounding. There was no way I was backing down now, not after everything we'd uncovered.

We moved again, past the main stage, where the lights had already been dimmed, casting long shadows across the seats. The theater had an unsettling feeling after hours, like something out of a dream that could turn into a nightmare at any second.

Ryan glanced toward the door that led to the dressing rooms. "We should check back here. If she's packing up or trying to make a run for it, it's the most logical place to find her."

I followed him, my nerves buzzing with every step. As we moved closer to the backstage area, the silence felt heavier. Each door we passed remained closed, the faint smells of stage makeup and dust lingering in the air.

"I just don't get it," I whispered, half to myself. "She had everything she could want. Why do this?"

Ryan's jaw tightened. "Greed. Jealousy. Fear. Take your pick. People do a lot worse for a lot less."

He was right, of course, but that didn't make it any easier to swallow. Katherine had manipulated Trent into following me, into creating a false narrative that she was being stalked—all to cover her own crimes. The very idea made my skin crawl.

We reached the door to Katherine's dressing room, and Ryan paused, one hand on the doorknob and the other on his gun. He glanced back at me one more time. "Stay behind me," he whispered.

I swallowed hard and nodded, standing back as he slowly pushed the door open.

Inside, Katherine's dressing room was brightly lit, unlike the dark, deserted theater. The vanity lights cast a warm, glowing halo across the room, illuminating the cluttered table littered with makeup brushes, half-empty bottles of perfume, and scraps of crumpled paper. But what caught my attention wasn't the chaos on the vanity—it was Katherine herself.

She was frantically shoving items into a large black suitcase, her hands moving with a feverish energy that betrayed her calm exterior. Her reflection in the mirror caught sight of us, and for a split second, her eyes widened with fear. But then, as if flipping a switch, her expression shifted into one of cool indifference.

"I'm sorry, but you're too late," she said, her voice steady as she zipped up the suitcase. "I'm leaving town. No more interviews, no more questions. No more autographs."

Ryan and I exchanged a glance, knowing this was it. He moved toward Katherine, his voice steady but firm. "Katherine, we need to talk. You're not going anywhere."

Katherine froze, her eyes darting toward the door like a trapped animal. "You don't understand," she stammered, taking a step back. "I didn't mean for it to happen like this. Kelly... she was always trying to take what was mine. And Charles—he threatened to tell everyone."

Ryan's voice remained calm, but his posture was tense. "Tell them what, Katherine? That you killed your sister?"

Her face twisted, a mixture of fear and anger flashing across it.

"She was stealing from me! She was ruining everything I worked for! Charles found out, and he said he was going to expose it all. I didn't have a choice."

"You always have a choice," Ryan said softly, taking another step closer.

For a moment, Katherine looked like she might bolt, but something in Ryan's eyes stopped her. She slumped against the vanity, defeated. "It wasn't supposed to end like this," she whispered. "None of it was."

Before either of us could say anything more, the sound of footsteps echoed in the hallway behind us. Another officer appeared at the door. Ryan nodded to him, and the officer moved forward to take Katherine into custody. Katherine didn't fight; she simply stood and allowed herself to be led out of the room, her head hanging low.

As the door closed behind them, I let out a long breath, the weight of everything we'd just uncovered slowly settling in. The truth was out. It was over.

Ryan stepped closer, his hand resting gently on my shoulder. "You alright?"

I nodded, though my legs felt like jelly. "I will be."

He smiled softly, his eyes full of concern. "Let's get out of here."

We walked in silence down the empty hallway, the remnants of the evening's tension still clinging to the air. By the time we stepped outside, the cold night air hit my skin like a shock, and I pulled my chef's coat tighter around me. But something else caught my attention, something magical.

White flakes of snow were gently falling, illuminated by the streetlights.

"Ryan," I whispered, staring up at the sky in disbelief. "It's snowing."

He turned to look, a grin spreading across his face as the

snowflakes drifted down around us. "What do you know?" he murmured, his voice low and full of warmth.

Despite everything—despite the chaos, the danger, and the tragedy that had unfolded—we stood there, watching the snow fall. The world felt quiet, peaceful, like a reset button had been pressed after all the madness.

Ryan wrapped an arm around me, pulling me close, and I leaned into him, resting my head against his chest. I could feel the steady rhythm of his heartbeat, the solid presence of him grounding me after the storm we'd weathered.

I looked up at him, his dark hair catching the snowflakes, his eyes soft as he watched me. My heart swelled with gratitude and love, emotions I hadn't fully processed until that moment. This man had been by my side through it all—protecting me, standing with me, supporting me, even when things had gotten messy.

"Thank you," I whispered, my voice barely audible over the soft patter of snow around us.

He smiled, leaning down to brush a kiss against my forehead. "You don't have to thank me."

I shook my head, my heart overflowing. "I do. For everything."

He kissed me again, slower this time, and for that brief moment, the world seemed to pause. It didn't matter what came next or what challenges we'd face. In that instant, it was just us—the snow falling softly, the warmth between us, and the quiet promise of everything still to come.

We stood there for a while longer, letting the peace of the night wash over us. The worst was behind us now. And somehow, against all odds, it was starting to feel like Christmas after all.

CHAPTER THIRTY-ONE

I woke to a world of white on Christmas morning. Snowflakes clung to the windowpanes, and outside, Sugar Creek was blanketed in a soft, shimmering layer of snow. It was a rare sight in our part of Texas, and for a moment, I just lay there, watching the flakes drift lazily down, feeling like I was inside a snow globe.

Cocoa, sensing I was awake, hopped onto the bed and nudged my arm with his cold nose, wagging his tail in excitement. "Good morning, mister," I whispered, scratching behind his ears. He gave a little huff of contentment, settling down beside me, his warm body pressed against my leg.

I could hear the faint sound of Cassie bustling around in the kitchen, probably making coffee. I stretched lazily and climbed out of bed, pulling on a thick sweater to ward off the chill. Cocoa trotted ahead of me as I made my way into the kitchen, where Cassie was pouring herself a cup of coffee. The rich smell filled the air, blending with the scent of pine from the Christmas tree in the corner of the room.

"Merry Christmas," Cassie said with a grin, holding out a steaming mug for me.

"Merry Christmas," I replied, taking a sip and sighing happily as the warmth spread through me. Cocoa sat by the door, watching us both with his usual patient expectancy.

Cassie nodded toward her bags by the door. "I'm about ready for the big trip. I checked the roads and they're clear all the way, which might be a blessing, or might be a curse."

I laughed. It was so unusual to see Cassie flustered by anything, but I knew that she was going to settle in just fine with Ty's family once she got there. There was a bittersweet pang in my chest at the thought of her leaving. "You'll have a great time. His family sounds fun."

She rolled her eyes playfully. "They are. Loud, but fun."

After a few minutes of chatting and finishing our coffee, we bundled up, grabbed our things, and headed outside to Cassie's truck. The snow crunched softly underfoot as Cocoa bounded ahead, his paws making tiny prints in the pristine white blanket.

"It's so beautiful," Cassie said as we carefully made our way to the truck. "I can't believe we actually got snow for Christmas."

"I know," I agreed, marveling at the winter wonderland that had transformed Sugar Creek overnight. "It's like something out of a movie."

Once we were all loaded up, Cocoa happily settled in between us, and Cassie started the engine. We pulled out slowly, navigating the snowy streets with care. As we drove, the town felt almost magical—the snow-covered rooftops, the twinkling holiday lights still glowing in windows, and the peaceful hush that only came with a fresh snowfall.

Cassie, Cocoa, and I stepped through the front door of Primrose House, greeted by the delicious scent of cinnamon, nutmeg, and something roasting in the oven. Christmas music drifted through the air, mingling with the sounds of laughter and lighthearted conversation from the kitchen.

Aunt Meg was at the center of it all, standing by the counter with a rolling pin in hand, her cheeks flushed from the warmth of the oven. Maria and her daughter, Daniela, were both working on pies, their hands covered in flour. The three of them were swaying and singing along to the cheerful tune playing on the radio, completely lost in the festive spirit.

"Hey! You made it just in time!" Aunt Meg called, her face lighting up as she spotted us. "Merry Christmas, girls! And Cocoa too, of course."

Cocoa gave a happy bark, his tail wagging as he trotted toward Aunt Meg for a scratch behind the ears.

"Merry Christmas!" Cassie and I chimed in unison, shedding our coats and scarves and placing the presents we'd brought on the counter. Cassie leaned in to give Aunt Meg a quick hug while I greeted Maria and Daniela.

"We're making pies, obviously," Maria said, holding up a tray of apple and pecan pies waiting to go into the oven. "But there's plenty of room for your roast too, Abby."

"Good, because it's about to steal the show," I teased, grabbing the ingredients for the roast from the counter where Aunt Meg had kindly set them out for me. "But first, let me grab a cup of that coffee."

Cassie laughed, already moving toward the coffeepot, which was sitting near the window. "I'm on it!"

I washed my hands and got to work prepping the roast, the sounds of happy chatter and Christmas carols filling the kitchen as I did. Maria and Daniela worked on the pies while Aunt Meg kept swaying and dancing, humming along to every song. The atmosphere was so warm and cozy that I almost forgot about all the chaos we'd gone through in the last few days.

"You know, it's been a while since we've had a Christmas morning like this," Aunt Meg said with a soft smile as she slid another pie into the oven. "I'm so glad you're here with us, Abby girl. Feels good, doesn't it?"

I nodded, smiling at her. "Yeah, it really does." I couldn't be happier to be in Sugar Creek with the people I loved.

Just as I was tying up the roast and getting ready to pop it into the oven, the doorbell rang, and Cocoa let out an excited bark, tail wagging as he ran to the door.

"That's probably Ty and Ryan," Cassie said with a grin, wiping her hands on a towel. "Let me get that."

She hurried to the door, and sure enough, Ty and Ryan stepped inside, both dusting snow from their coats.

"Merry Christmas, y'all!" Ty said, his voice booming with joy as he hugged Cassie and handed her a sprig of mistletoe, then leaned in for a long kiss. "Figured we couldn't show up without something festive!"

"Merry Christmas!" Aunt Meg, Maria, and Daniela called out in unison, the energy in the kitchen instantly becoming even more festive with the arrival of the two men.

Ryan smiled at me, crossing the room to where I stood by the stove. "Merry Christmas, Abby," he said softly, his brown eyes twinkling as he leaned in for a quick kiss. "You've outdone yourself again. This kitchen smells amazing."

"Merry Christmas," I replied, feeling the warmth of his presence wash over me. "You're just in time—we're about to get this roast going."

Cassie poured Ty and Ryan cups of coffee as the kitchen buzzed with chatter and soon enough, everyone had settled into a comfortable rhythm. Cocoa curled up in the corner, watching the flurry of activity with contentment, his nose twitching now and then at the delicious smells coming from the oven.

After a quick breakfast and a few small gifts exchanged, Cassie and Ty made their way to the door, suitcases in hand, ready for the trip to Dallas. Cocoa watched them with a curious tilt of his head, almost as if he was asking if he could come too. I patted him with a laugh. "You're staying with me this time, buddy."

"Drive safe," Aunt Meg called from the kitchen, waving a floury hand at them.

Cassie gave me a quick hug. "I'll see you in a few days. Try to stay out of trouble, okay?"

I smiled, squeezing her back. "No promises."

Ty grinned, pulling Cassie toward him as they headed out the door. "Merry Christmas, y'all. We'll call when we get there."

"Merry Christmas!" we all called as the door closed behind them, and just like that, the house grew a little quieter.

Ryan stepped over to me, his expression soft but serious. "Hey, Abby. Can we talk for a second?"

I felt a little flutter in my stomach as I nodded and followed him out into the hallway. He glanced back at the kitchen, where the others were still chatting and cleaning up, before turning to me, his expression more tender than I'd seen in days.

"I've been thinking about everything," he started, his voice low. "About Trent, the car, the whole stalker situation... and how I didn't believe you when you said someone was following you."

My heart softened at his words, and I could see the genuine regret in his eyes. He took my hands, his thumb brushing softly over my knuckles.

"I'm really sorry, Abby," he continued. "I should have trusted you. You've got good instincts, and I let my frustration with the case cloud my judgment. I hope you know that I'll always have your back."

I smiled, feeling the weight of the last few days lift just a little. "You do, Ryan. And I get it—it was a lot to handle. But thank you for saying that."

He reached into his coat pocket, pulling out a small velvet box. "I wanted to give you something. Something that's practical but special too." He opened the box, revealing a pair of simple yet beautiful pearl earrings. "I figured you could wear these even while you're cooking."

I blinked, surprised by the thoughtful gesture. "Ryan... they're beautiful."

"They're just a little something," he said softly. "To remind you how much you mean to me. And how much I love you."

I felt my cheeks warm as I looked up at him, overwhelmed by the kindness and love in his gesture. "Thank you," I whispered, standing on tiptoe to kiss him gently. "I love them. And I love you, too, Ryan."

He smiled, pulling me close. "Merry Christmas, Abby."

"Merry Christmas," I whispered as our lips met and I felt it down to my toes. This man was a keeper, despite the occasional frustration I had to endure.

We rejoined the others in the living room, where Aunt Meg had already lit the fireplace, the soft crackle of the flames adding a cozy warmth to the room. Maria and Daniela had settled on the couch with cups of hot chocolate, and Cocoa had claimed his spot near the fire, content to watch the snowflakes drift lazily past the window.

Ryan and I sat together on the loveseat by the fire, our fingers laced together as we gazed out at the snowy landscape beyond the window. The world outside was peaceful, blanketed in white, and for the first time in days, I felt a sense of calm wash over me.

"What do you think is ahead for us?" I asked quietly, my head resting on Ryan's shoulder.

He glanced down at me, his expression soft and thoughtful. "I don't know," he admitted, his voice low. "But whatever it is, we'll face it together."

I smiled, closing my eyes as I let the warmth of the fire and the comfort of his words wrap around me. The future was uncertain, but for now, I was surrounded by love, friendship, and the promise of a new beginning.

And that was enough.

ABBY'S HOLIDAY DIVINITY

Like Abby says, this is a finicky dessert! You'll need a lot of patience, a candy thermometer, and a stand mixer to get it right. Good luck!

INGREDIENTS
- 2½ cups sugar
- ½ cup light corn syrup
- ½ cup water
- 2 large egg whites
- 1 teaspoon vanilla extract
- ½ cup chopped pecans or walnuts (optional)
- Pinch of salt

DIRECTIONS
• In a heavy-bottomed saucepan, combine sugar, corn syrup, and water.

• Cook over medium heat, stirring constantly until the sugar dissolves and the mixture comes to a boil.

• Attach a candy thermometer to the saucepan.

• Continue cooking without stirring until the syrup reaches

260°F (127°C), known as the hard ball stage. This usually takes about 10 minutes.

• While the syrup is cooking, beat the egg whites and a pinch of salt in a large mixing bowl using an electric mixer on medium speed until stiff peaks form.

• Once the syrup reaches 260°F, remove it from the heat.

• Slowly pour the hot syrup in a thin, steady stream into the beaten egg whites while continuing to beat on medium speed. Be careful to avoid splattering.

• Add the vanilla extract to the mixture.

• Increase the mixer speed to high.

• Beat the mixture until it loses its gloss and holds its shape, which may take about 5-6 minutes. The mixture should be thick but still spoonable.

• Gently fold in the chopped nuts if you're using them.

• Using two spoons, drop spoonfuls of the mixture onto a baking sheet lined with wax paper or parchment paper.

• Alternatively, you can use a piping bag for more uniform shapes.

• Allow the divinity to cool and set at room temperature until firm. This can take about 1 hour.

Festive Eggnog

INGREDIENTS

4 cups whole milk

5 large eggs

½ cup sugar

1 teaspoon vanilla extract

½ teaspoon ground nutmeg

¼ teaspoon ground cinnamon

Optional: ½ cup heavy cream (for extra richness)

Optional: ½ to 1 cup rum, bourbon, or brandy

DIRECTIONS

• In a medium saucepan, whisk together the eggs and sugar until thoroughly combined and slightly frothy.

• Gradually pour in the milk while continuing to whisk to ensure a smooth mixture.

• Place the saucepan over medium heat.

• Stir constantly until the mixture thickens slightly and reaches 160°F (71°C) on a candy thermometer. This step pasteurizes the eggs for safety. **Do not let the mixture boil**.

• Remove the saucepan from the heat.

- Stir in the vanilla extract, ground nutmeg, and ground cinnamon.
- If you're using heavy cream, stir it in now for a richer texture.
- Allow the mixture to cool to room temperature.
- If adding alcohol, mix it in after the mixture has cooled.
- Transfer the eggnog to a pitcher or airtight container.
- Refrigerate for at least 2 hours or until well chilled.
- Before serving, stir the eggnog to ensure it's well mixed.
- Pour into glasses and garnish with a sprinkle of nutmeg or a cinnamon stick if desired.

Snickerdoodles

INGREDIENTS

1½ cups sugar, divided

½ cup (1 stick) butter, softened

½ cup shortening

2 large eggs

2¾ cups all-purpose flour

2 teaspoons cream of tartar

1 teaspoon baking soda

¼ teaspoon salt

2 teaspoons ground cinnamon

DIRECTIONS

• Preheat your oven to 400°F (200°C).

• Line baking sheets with parchment paper or lightly grease them.

• In a large mixing bowl, combine ½ cup of the sugar, butter, and shortening.

• Beat with an electric mixer on medium speed until light and fluffy.

• Add the eggs one at a time, beating well after each addition.

• In a separate bowl, whisk together the flour, cream of tartar, baking soda, and salt.

• Gradually add the dry ingredients to the wet ingredients.

• Mix until just combined and a soft dough forms.

• In a small bowl, mix the remaining 1 cup of sugar with the ground cinnamon.

• Roll the dough into balls about 1 to 1½ inches in diameter.

• Roll each dough ball in the cinnamon-sugar mixture until fully coated.

• Place the coated dough balls on the prepared baking sheets, spacing them about 2 inches apart.

• Bake for 8 to 10 minutes or until the edges are set and the tops are crackled.

ABOUT NOVA WALSH

Author Nova Walsh writes culinary cozy mysteries full of humor, shenanigans, and friendships that last a lifetime. She mixes in a healthy dose of amateur sleuthing, some slow-burn romance, and a pinch of comedy in every book she writes.

Nova is a former chef/caterer who still loves to cook but loves to write even more. She's an enthusiastic, if not totally successful gardener and loves travel, wine, and hanging out with friends.

Nova lives in central Texas with her husband, son, and two delightfully crazy pups. When she isn't writing, she's often cooking, gardening, hiking, or reading a good book with a pup by her side.

You can contact Nova at nova@novawalsh.com